FRAYED BOND

KAYDENCE SNOW

Editing by Kirstin Andrews

Cover by Fantastical Ink

kaydencesnow.com

ONE

The immaculately dressed woman behind the reception desk frowned slightly at her computer screen, then clicked away at a few more keys.

"I'm so sorry," she said, looking up. "There seems to be a problem with the system."

I kept my snarky remark to myself and forced a polite reply. "Yes. As I said, there seems to have been an issue with it since the start of the semester. I really need this figured out. I'm worried about how it might affect my final grade."

I thought that everyone employed by Bradford Hills Institute was ridiculously smart, but this woman appeared to be an exception.

"Yes, I understand. The issue is wider than that." She clacked a bit on her keyboard again before returning her attention to me. "Our entire school network seems to be having issues this morning. I won't be able to access the appropriate database to look into your issue until they fix it."

I sighed but stayed put. My student log-in showed I was enrolled in the third-level strategic management unit, but none of my assignment grades or feedback were showing up.

The lecturer said he was inputting them the same as every student's, and no one else in the class was having issues. I'd been trying to get this fixed for months, but every time I emailed admin, they replied that it was fixed. But it wasn't!

My one lecture for the day was done, and I'd just come from lunch. I had nothing else going on for the rest of the day and wasn't leaving until this mess was cleared up.

"How long is that going to take?" I glanced down the length of the admin counter. There were five admin staff taking calls, speaking to people as they came up. A line had begun to form behind me.

"I don't know. I'm sorry." She seemed genuine, and I felt bad for thinking she was dumb moments earlier. "A Variant with a tech ability is looking into it, so it'll be faster than any human would need to fix it, but I just don't know. I can take down your details and make sure the issue is passed on to the appropriate team."

"No, thank you." I gave her an extra-polite smile. "I've tried that several times. I'm just going to wait, if that's OK."

"Your call." She shrugged and smoothed her hand over her impeccably smooth hair.

I made my way over to the seating area, my Manolo boots clicking on the marble. Bradford Hills Institute was one of the oldest schools in the country and accepted almost exclusively students with Variant DNA. About 18 percent of the world population had the gene. It didn't automatically mean you'd end up with some kind of supernatural ability, but it was a precursor.

The campus's rolling hills and intricate architecture hinted at a time long gone. But the admin building was a more recent addition; its aesthetic was the epitome of modern and sleek.

I sat on one of the leather couches and took out my

laptop. The coffee table was way too low, so I balanced the computer on my knees and attempted to do some studying while I waited.

My neck started to ache after about fifteen minutes, so I abandoned that plan and took my phone out to scan social media instead. Despite my determination to wait, my patience was already wearing thin. Maybe I could hunt down this Variant with the tech ability and transfer him or her some Light.

I may not have been that good at it yet, but I was still a Vital. Surely some extra Light could help.

A blood test was part of the admissions process at Bradford Hills, and my parents had enrolled me when I was twelve. I'd known from an early age I had Variant DNA, and I'd discovered a few years ago I was a Vital. I had access to the pure, unadulterated power that fueled a Variant's ability—the Light. A Variant with super speed could cover the same distance four times over that a professional human athlete could in the same amount of time. A Variant with super speed *and* a Vital could run from DC to New York while those first two dudes were skipping around that track.

The elevators at the far end of the lobby dinged, and several people piled out. It had been a busy fifteen minutes, with people being sent away by the admin staff and others coming and going through the lobby. Most of the people from the elevator headed outside, pulling scarves and sweaters in tightly. It was spring, but the windy day had a bite to it.

One man didn't head for the front doors though; he made his way to the reception desk, casually leaned on the end, and spoke to the woman seated there.

I kept my phone in front of my face, my thumb mechanically scrolling, but I wasn't even remotely looking at the screen. Because Tyler Gabriel—with his shirtsleeves rolled up and his perfectly tailored pants hugging his ass—was leaning over, and I had an unobstructed view and nowhere to be.

Half the students at BHI, and a good portion of the staff too, had crushes on the admissions counselor. He threw his head back and laughed, shoving some of his messy hair out of his face as the woman he was talking to blushed.

I bit my lip lightly, raking my eyes up and down his body. *Man*, I needed to get laid. I was a year and a half away from graduating—a college-level qualification—and the workload was murder on my social life.

The couch cushion dipped as someone plonked down in the seat next to me. Startled, I fumbled with my phone and nearly dropped it.

"Sorry. Didn't mean to scare you," an amused male voice said to my right.

"Oh! No, you didn't. It's OK." I cleared my throat, then crossed my legs as I tucked my phone away. I avoided even glancing in the guy's direction, trying to play it cool.

Whatever the conversation was at the admin desk ended, and Tyler walked across the lobby toward the elevators.

"Maybe I should stop wearing ties to work," the guy to my right said, making me turn to look at him properly.

He was in a charcoal checked suit and crisp white shirt, with a burnt-orange tie that was a few shades darker than his amber eyes. His dark brown hair was short and styled in neat waves. His bow-shaped lips curved in a barely restrained smile.

"What?" I asked lamely. What had he even said? Something about a tie? Fucking hell, why were all the men in this building so hot. It was distracting.

"I was just wondering if you'd check *me* out like that if I lost the tie," he said, his smile teasing, his gaze flirty.

"I don't know what you're talking about." I sat up a little straighter.

"I'm talking about how you were just checking out Gabe. I mean, I get it—he's a good-looking dude. But you were practically drooling."

"I was *not*." I gave him a frown, but his smirk only deepened.

"You've got a little something . . ." He rubbed at the corner of his mouth with one manicured finger, and I reflexively wiped at my face before I realized what he was doing.

"Stop," I huffed and smacked him on the shoulder.

He chuckled and held his hands up in surrender.

We fell into silence for a few moments, and I forced myself to take some measured breaths. Between being busted perving and being taken by surprise by how hot he was, my heart was working in overdrive.

I couldn't stop my gaze from flicking over to him. He had his phone out, but I had a feeling he was paying about as much attention to it as I had been to mine earlier. Our eyes kept meeting.

I twisted to face him fully. "Don't lose the tie."

"No?" He raised his eyebrows.

"It brings out the warm amber in your eyes. Makes it harder to look away. Plus, it really ties the outfit together. Is this Brioni?" I rubbed the soft wool of his suit jacket sleeve. Now that I had my shit together, I was intentionally flirting.

"It is." He sounded impressed. "You have a good eye."

"Did you just compliment yourself?"

He shrugged. "How can we expect anyone to be into us if we're not into ourselves?"

"True," I conceded, my hand still on his sleeve. I couldn't seem to remove it.

"But I'd be happy to compliment you. I have at least a dozen ready to go."

"A dozen? I didn't realize I made such an impression."

"Oh, you make one hell of an impression." His voice dropped an octave, making our conversation feel private, intimate—even in a cavernous lobby with at least a dozen other people around. "Those hazel eyes of yours, for one. They remind me of a meadow at sunset—warm brown and soft green. They're beautiful, even if they were checking out another man."

"*Stop*," I chastised, but it didn't have any bite to it, considering it was delivered through a massive grin.

"Your hair looks as soft as silk and shines like the sun reflecting on cool water."

I mentally thanked myself for taking the time to wash my hair that morning. "So, you're into blondes then."

"I'm into this blonde." He reached out and took a strand of hair between his fingers, stroking it gently.

"Miss Roy." The sound of my last name almost startled me. I hadn't even heard the admin lady walk up. "The tech issue is resolved. I can help you with your glitch now."

"Oh, great!" I got to my feet, the amber-eyed hottie following suit. "Thank you. I'll be right there."

She nodded and marched her way back to the desk.

"I'd better get moving." The hottie checked his expensive-looking watch. "I'm already late. Not a good look for my second week on the job."

"You work here?" I asked, putting my laptop back into my bag.

He pointed to the ceiling. "Two floors up."

"I thought you were waiting for reception or something."

"Nope. Just wanted to talk to you."

"Well, I hope it was worth potentially losing your job."

"It absolutely was, Miss Roy." He flashed me a flirty smile, not looking in any rush to get back to work.

"Well, that's not fair. You know my name and I don't know yours." *Or your number*. Would he give me his number now that he knew I was a student? Would he even still be interested? He was still flirting so . . .

"Leon Livingston." He held his hand out. "An absolute pleasure to meet you."

Was it just me, or did he put a tiny little bit of emphasis on the word *pleasure*?

"Oriana Roy." I placed my hand in his, and he shook it.

His hand was warm, his grip sure but gentle. It felt as if he were hugging me; a warm feeling spread through my body, even though only our hands touched.

I really wanted to kiss him. I'd never been so attracted to someone in my life. Tyler Gabriel was hot, but now that I was looking at this man properly, now that I'd spoken to him, Tyler had nothing on Leon Livingston.

I had to shoot my shot.

I cleared my throat. "Hey, would you like to maybe—"

"Yes." He cut me off with an infectious smile. We were still holding hands, neither of us making a move to step back.

I smiled back, my cheeks heating. I didn't blush often or easily, but this guy was making me feel all kinds of things.

"Livingston!" someone barked from near the elevators, and Leon's eyes widened.

"Shit," he muttered, dropping my hand and walking backward. "Gotta run. I'll find you, Oriana Roy."

Before I could point out that we hadn't even exchanged numbers or anything, he was in the elevator and gone.

Suddenly, everything seemed a little duller. But I was confident Leon and I would cross paths again. I'd make sure of it.

I couldn't completely wipe the smile off my face as I floated over to reception.

Everything was coming up Oriana; the issue with my class was resolved within minutes, and I skipped out of the building. I couldn't even be mad about the delay—it had allowed me to meet Leon. If anything, I was thankful for whatever that technical issue was.

"What's got you smiling like that?" Crystal, one of my roomies, asked as I let myself into our res hall room.

"I met a guy," I sighed, fully aware of how sappy I sounded.

Crystal smacked her physics book closed and dropped the heavy tome on the couch next to her. "Well, this is way more interesting than my physics assignment." She sat forward and put her curly black hair up in a messy bun. "Spill."

"Is Ebony here?" I asked, pulling my boots and coat off. Our third roomie would want all the details too.

"Yeah, but so's her Bond." Crystal bugged her eyes out, and we both glanced at the door on the left—her bedroom. As if waiting for the cue, a chorus of moans came through the door.

Crystal grabbed her phone and turned the volume up on her music.

"It's the middle of the afternoon." I chuckled, sitting down next to Crystal and crossing my legs under me.

"Yeah, but they're Bonded." Crystal shrugged, and I rolled my eyes and nodded.

Ebony was a Vital like me, and she had two Bonded Variants. She'd met Derek and Kylie at a mixer at the beginning of the year. They'd been dating and getting to know each other for months while training. Bradford Hills Institute provided coaching and training for new Bonds so the Vitals could learn how to transfer Light in a controlled manner and the Variants could learn to handle their newly supercharged powers.

It was apparently a fine balance, because once you found your Bonded, the Light made you want to jump each other to solidify the connection. It was not uncommon to hear Ebony having threesomes in her room lately. The training was going well, and they were fully giving in to their hormonal and Light-driven urges.

What if Leon is my Variant? The thought smacked me across the face. I'd been so wrapped up in the warm, fuzzy feelings of our meet-cute I'd barely had any coherent thoughts. But the sounds coming from Ebony's room pushed my brain to finally make the connection.

"OK, spill," Crystal demanded again. "Who's the hottie?"

"Holy shit, what if he's my Variant?" I blurted.

Crystal laughed. "I'm gonna need some context here."

"Yeah, fair enough." I laughed along. I told her about meeting Leon, going into detail about every part of our interaction.

"So, you think he could be your Bonded?" Crystal asked, fully invested.

"I don't know. I just . . . girl, I have never been so attracted to a guy in my life."

"And he's definitely a Variant? Maybe he's just an insanely hot dude."

"Valid point." I chewed the inside of my cheek. "I'm

getting ahead of myself, aren't I? I mean, he didn't even ask for my number. Maybe he's just a flirt."

Crystal shrugged. "He could be. Or he could be your Bonded Variant. I guess time will tell."

"Yeah, you're right."

"See if he walks the walk. If he's really interested, he'll find you, like he said."

"True . . ." I wanted to argue, point out that I knew the building and the floor he worked on and he only knew I was a student at a massive school. I mean, we had three libraries on campus—three! It would be much easier for me to find him.

But Crystal had a point. Maybe I was just desperate to find my Bonded and seeing signs that weren't there. Most Vitals found their Variants by the time they were out of their teens. I was nearly twenty-two and getting antsy.

Crystal got back to her assignment, and I got up to make a snack in our tiny little kitchenette, mentally giving myself a pep talk.

Leon would find me. If we were connected by the Light itself, he wouldn't be able to help it. I had to trust in the divine wisdom of the raw, unfiltered power coursing through my veins.

And if he wasn't mine, well, there was no rule against having a little no-strings-attached fun with a hot dude before a young Vital found her Variants.

TWO

A week passed without so much as a messenger pigeon from Leon. So much for his promise to find me. Maybe he was just a flirt with no follow-through. He probably didn't even work at Bradford Hills Institute. *Whatever*. We'd had only one brief conversation with intense eye contact. There were plenty of other insanely hot, well-dressed guys with mesmerizing smiles out there.

But I couldn't put the asshole out of my mind.

The people around me started getting to their feet, snapping me out of my brooding thoughts. I'd missed the last ten minutes of the lecture entirely—not that I'd been paying the best attention for the rest of it.

I slapped my book closed and shoved my stuff into my bag as the theater-style seats thunked up around me, the lecture hall clearing out.

"Just go and see if you can find the guy already." Ebony chuckled as she led the way to the exit. "If nothing else, you can put yourself out of this distracted misery."

"I am not miserable," I huffed, falling into step beside her. "Nor am I distracted."

"Yeah, OK, then you won't mind telling me what happened on last night's episode of *Buffy*?" She flipped her long red hair over her shoulder and gave me a smug smile.

I pressed my lips together and glared at her as we followed the stream of other students up the hall. My roomies and I had a weekly Tuesday-night ritual. We took turns cooking dinner before settling in for a few episodes of the classic show. We were on season three. Last week's episode had ended on a brutal cliffy, and I'd been *gagging* for the next one, but Ebony was right. I'd zoned out for the entire thing, obsessing over a guy!

Conceding defeat, I sighed and hung my head.

She placed a gentle hand on my arm. "No douchebag is worth this, Oriana. You deserve better."

"Thank you." I pulled her in for a hug, which she kept brief when she realized she was running late for her next class.

I waved her off and she rushed through the door, letting in a fresh gust of air. I hung back to dig my sunglasses out of my bag before going out.

The door didn't quite close after Ebony, as someone grabbed it on their way into the building.

My hand froze at the zip on my bag—what was I even looking for?

It was him. Leon's cheeks were pink from the cold, his hair windswept. He smoothed the wayward locks down as he glanced up the stairs and down the corridors.

When his eyes landed on me, he went still. It wasn't the "oh shit" kind of still that involved wide eyes and a grimace when you spotted someone you wanted to avoid. It looked like a grounding kind of stillness—as if calm had settled into his bones as he found what he was looking for.

Me?

He walked over, his tan loafers eating up the distance between us.

"Hey," he said, stuffing his hands into his pockets.

I readjusted my bag on my shoulder and cleared my throat. "Uh, hey. Leon, right?"

I internally rolled my eyes at myself. *Leon, right?* As if I hadn't been doodling his name on my study notes all damn week like a middle schooler.

"Yes, Oriana Roy, I'm Leon." He smiled wider, then schooled his features into a more serious expression. "I hope you don't mind me showing up at your lecture like this. I nearly missed you. I was running late because of this meeting, and then I had to get across campus and—"

"You came here looking for me?" I cut into his rambling as something warm settled in my chest. Maybe he hadn't been able to find me until now.

"Yes." He looked a bit sheepish, glancing away for a second. "I hope I'm not coming across as a creep or something. I know I should've taken the unanswered messages as a hint, but honestly, I can't stop thinking about you, and I had to try one last time, face-to-face. Shit, that sounded really fucking creepy, didn't it?"

"You can't stop thinking about me?" I was positive my eyes had taken on a heart shape and I was smiling like a fool.

He visibly relaxed at my reaction and stepped a little closer.

"Are you kidding me? I can hardly concentrate I think about you so much. You're even more beautiful than I remember." He tucked a strand of hair behind my ear with a feather-light touch. A shiver skittered up my spine, but I was overheated, not cold.

"I've been thinking about you too. To be honest, I was

considering going over to the admin building to try to bump into you again."

We both chuckled, and he nudged my shoulder with his. "I guess I bumped into you first."

"Wait." His earlier rambling registered in my mind. "What messages?"

"The ones I sent you on the school network. I work in the marketing department, so I don't have access to students' personal details, which is why I couldn't find your number, although that probably would've been unethical anyway."

"Oh my god," I muttered as I grabbed my phone and opened the BHI app. All students and staff had profiles on the school's network. It was primarily used to track classes, grades, course updates, and school assignments, but it did have a chat feature. No one ever used the chat feature. I swiped over to it and found multiple notifications from "Leon L. (Mktg.)."

I put my phone away without reading them. I had the real thing right in front of me; no way was I going to waste time staring at my phone.

"I didn't see them," I admitted, and he grinned.

"You have no idea what a relief this is for my ego."

I couldn't help laughing, then I smacked him on the arm. "Why didn't you try social media? I tried to find you, but I couldn't." Ebony, Crystal, and I had all tried, on various platforms.

"Oh, I don't know why I didn't think of that!" He looked genuinely disappointed in himself. "Probably because I don't go on socials much anymore. And all my profiles are private."

Someone opened the front door on their way out of the building, letting in another cool gust of wind. I'd been so consumed with our conversation that the surroundings had completely melted away. Everyone had moved on to their next classes or other obligations, leaving the area empty and quiet.

"Would you like to get some lunch?" Leon asked, glancing around.

"Yes, I'd love that." I didn't hesitate. I wanted to keep talking to him, keep looking at his impossibly handsome face, maybe even touch him a bit more.

We went off campus for lunch, taking a walk into town and settling into a cozy corner of a café. I got the savory crepes and he had fritters, and the conversation flowed effortlessly. He told me about his entry-level marketing position with Bradford Hills Institute. I told him about my studies and plans to eventually start my own ethical shoe brand.

We talked books, and movies, and even fashion.

When I realized it was midafternoon, I asked: "Don't you have to get back to work? I didn't realize what time it was."

"Nah." He waved it off. "Not working today."

"Why were you on campus on your day off?" I chuckled.

"That's where you were." His expression was open, honest, a little flirty.

"Why do I get the feeling you're going to be trouble?" I teased, feeling slightly giddy.

He leaned forward on the table and gave me a sinful look. "I can be as much trouble as you'd like me to be."

I held his gaze for a beat, glanced down at his teasing lips. I really wanted to kiss him.

"What does that even mean?" I laughed and was relieved to see he laughed right along with me—an easy, free sound. He wasn't the kind of guy to get pissy at a girl for teasing him about his flirting.

"I don't know." He shook his head, mirth still shaking his shoulders. "Let's get out of here."

He got to his feet, dropped several bills on the table, and held his hand out for me.

I let him pull me up. "Where are we going?"

"Did you know that BHI has three libraries?" he whispered conspiratorially as we left the café.

"I've been studying there for over ten years, so yeah, I did know that."

"Ah, but I bet you haven't spent much time in the Aldrich Library." He tucked my hand into the crook of his elbow, and our steps matched as we headed back to campus.

"No . . ." That library was more for the public and visiting lectures and museum displays. The students and faculty did actual study and research in the other two.

"Did you know that last year they acquired several of René Caovilla's early sketches?"

"No way." I gaped at him. How the hell had I missed this? The shoe designer was one of my heroes.

"Yep. They're part of a collection of notable items from past BHI students." Leon grinned, and we picked up our pace.

We talked more on the way there. He told me that he grew up in New York and had planned to attend BHI but ended up going to a school in France. I told him about my brother who worked for Melior Group. Leon was curious about that, asking questions about the elite private security firm that employed almost exclusively Variants. I was just as curious about what it was like to live in France. I'd never been, and he promised to take me . . . in French!

Who *was* this guy?

At the Aldrich Library, we took our time looking at all the gorgeous sketches of shoes by the legendary designer before moving through the rest of the display. Leon didn't seem impatient at all, and once again, I lost track of time. We spoke quietly in the hushed building, weaving through the displays, not so subtly brushing past each other, letting our hands linger in touches that left me breathless on more than one occasion. I'd flirted with plenty of guys before, but it had never been so fun, so . . . *charged* as it was with Leon.

We ended up having dinner together too—dumplings at a hole-in-the-wall place just off campus—and it was dark by the time he walked me back to my res hall, my backpack slung over his shoulder, our steps almost comically slow. I didn't want this day to end, but a yawn I couldn't hold back gave away how tired I was.

"As much as I hate to say goodbye, you should get some rest." Leon turned to face me at the door to the building.

"Sorry, it's been a big week. Aren't you tired?"

"Nope. I'm positively invigorated. I think I might go to the gym after this."

"Jerk." I smacked his chest, and he caught my hand before it could drop, then held it in place with his.

"I had an amazing afternoon with you, Oriana," he said, his expression turning a little more serious. "And I'd like to see you again."

"I'd like that too. This was the best first date I've ever been on."

"This was a date?" He raised his eyebrows, something between hope and uncertainty swimming in his gaze.

"Yes." I nodded decisively.

"Well then, we'd better end it like a date." He leaned in, gently brushing my hair off my shoulder.

My lips parted, my body so ready for what was clearly about to happen.

"I'm going to kiss you now," he whispered, his nose brushing mine. This close I could make out the smell I'd been getting hints of all day—leather and tangerine.

"You better," I breathed, and his lips pressed against mine in the softest, most tender kiss I'd ever had. I sighed, wrapping my arms around his neck. I was melting, about to be a literal puddle of giddy hormones at this man's feet.

One of his arms wrapped around my waist, holding me close, and the other hand settled at my neck, his thumb caressing my cheek. We kissed for a long time, our lips moving languidly, tongues caressing gently. It was an all-consuming kiss, the kind that made everything else fall away.

We pulled away naturally, breathing each other's air.

I ducked my head as I released a steadying breath. My lips tingled, and I didn't want to leave the warmth of his arms. *Holy shit*, he was a good kisser.

"Why do I get the feeling you're going to be trouble?" Leon's voice was low, husky, as he repeated my sentiment from earlier in the day.

"Oh, baby, I can be as much trouble as you'd like me to be." I grinned up at him before going in for another kiss.

THREE

My skirt swished around my thighs as Ebony, Crystal, and I walked up the gravel driveway of one of the most impressive mansions in Bradford Hills. Our steps matched perfectly, in rhythm with the bass pumping from somewhere up ahead.

"I really should be studying. Not partying," Crystal grumbled. "I'm way behind in Quantitative Modeling."

"That's exactly why you should be partying," Ebony stated, as if it was the most obvious thing in the world.

"Yeah, your brain works better when it's rested. Let's just have some fun." I shook my shoulders and threw her a wink.

She leveled a narrow-eyed look at me, then Ebony. "Whatever. I could use a drink. Maybe I can get laid too. That would help me feel rested for more study."

"Oh yes, that definitely works." Ebony nodded sagely.

"Yep. Can confirm. Although not lately." I fought to keep the grin off my face. Leon and I were officially together. I suspected he might be my Variant, but we hadn't broached the subject, and we hadn't slept together yet. All I knew was that I found it ridiculously easy to transfer Light to him—a sign that we had a Bond—and that I *really* liked him.

He'd been away for work for two weeks now, and I missed him like crazy, but I was still riding the high of our newly official relationship status. He was coming home on Monday. Two more sleeps! It sucked that he had to be away so early in our relationship, but he was new in the job and not in a position to say no to a trip that had been planned before we even met.

We made our way up to the ornate front doors and let ourselves in. The music got louder, mingling with the sound of people talking and laughing, having a great time.

"Hey, girls!" Dorothy Vanderford came skipping down the stairs, the giant chandelier making her black hair shine. As usual, I admired her outfit. Girl knew how to dress, and she was in a skin-tight bright pink dress and black fishnets.

"Hey, Dot!" We shared hugs as her twin brother, Charlie, joined us. We greeted him just as warmly but left out the hugs.

He nodded and smiled back. Charlie was Dot's Vital—a rare sibling Bond—and the pair were well-known on campus. It didn't hurt that they were loaded and their cousin threw the most epic parties.

"So, is your cousin around?" Crystal craned her neck to look toward the back of the house, where most of the noise was coming from.

"Somewhere." Dot waved her hand dismissively while Ebony and I hid our chuckles behind our hands.

Crystal was serious about getting laid then. Ethan "Kid" Paul—one of the residents of the house we currently stood in—may have been two years younger than her, but the guy had a certain reputation on campus. If she was already seeking him out, she was determined to have a good time.

"Drinks?" Dot grinned and led us through the house. It was more crowded in the spacious kitchen and living area, where the dance floor was set up. We lost Crystal on our way through. I spotted her walking up to Kid in the kitchen as we headed for the backyard. He was leaning against the kitchen island, surrounded by a group of people. Dude was massive—taller than everyone in the room and really testing the fabric of the T-shirt he was wearing. I had no idea why they called him Kid, because it didn't fit him one bit.

Out on the back patio, a bar was set up near the pool. That's where we lost Ebony. Derek and Kylie were sitting around a firepit, and she beelined for them without even getting a drink. Kylie handed her a beer before Ebony settled on Derek's lap.

Dot, Charlie, and I got some drinks and chatted for a while, but I lost track of them too. I knew a lot of the people at the party—we'd all been going to Bradford Hills Institute since we were kids. So I milled about, chatting with friends, dancing for a bit, having another few drinks.

I was standing at the far end of the pool, talking to some friends, when the night took an interesting turn.

There were a bunch of drunk dudes play-wrestling on the lawn beyond the pool. No one was paying them much attention, and they weren't hurting anyone—just having some fun. One of them had enhanced speed and was laying the others out as they tried to catch him. A tall guy wearing a backward baseball cap managed to grab speedy's T-shirt. It wasn't enough to stop him, but it threw him off-balance and off-course.

He came shooting through our group before anyone even noticed what was happening. Two of my friends went straight into the pool, limbs flailing, water splashing everywhere. Speedy managed to stop himself right at the edge and teetered over the water on his toes.

He'd clipped my shoulder when he barreled into our group. I spun on the spot, my feet tangling, and started to tip backward into the pool. Squeezing my eyes shut, I hoped I wouldn't smack into my friends already in there.

But instead of the jarring splash of cold water on my back, something warm appeared at my front. An arm wrapped around me to reverse my trajectory, and I fell forward—right onto a man.

We landed with an *oof*, him on his back on the grass and me on his chest. I smacked my nose against his collarbone and winced. The pain shot through my face and made my eyes water.

"Shit, shit. You OK?"

I felt his words and his breaths in his chest and looked up into the most arresting eyes I'd ever seen. They were brown—the most common eye color—but they seemed to shine in the dim glow of the string lights above the pool.

His arms remained banded around me, and I had the sudden urge to lower my head to the crook of his neck and inhale the sweet, woodsy smell that was making me a little dizzy. Or maybe that was the knock to the head.

I inhaled again, mouth watering at the scent of vanilla and that masculine woodsy undertone.

Fuck, what the hell was I even thinking? I had a boyfriend.

I scrambled to get out of his arms, and he released me immediately, but he didn't go far. Instead, he reached out and helped me to my feet.

No one was even looking in our direction. They were all busy getting the other two out of the pool.

"I'm boyfriend!" I blurted, way too loudly.

My savior held up his hands, palms out, and then stuffed them into the pockets of his dark jeans. "Hi, boyfriend. I'm Mason." He chuckled. "That's an unusual name. What's the origin?"

He was a smartass, but he made me smile, his easy nature soothing the jittery, adrenaline-fueled fluttering in my chest and belly.

I took a deep breath before responding. "Sorry, hi. I'm Oriana. Ignore that weird outburst. I . . . don't know what that was. What I meant to say was I *have* a boyfriend."

"Oriana." His mouth formed the syllables of my name as if he was tasting it and liked the flavor. Then his lips pulled up into a wide, mesmerizing smile. I found myself returning it, unable to stop my facial muscles from forming the expression. Just as powerless to stop it as I was to stop the blush warming my cheeks.

It took me way too long to realize we were just standing there grinning at each other like a couple of deranged clowns.

"What the fuck?" I muttered, looking away and shaking my head to clear it.

"You all right?" Mason took a step closer, his smile replaced by a look of concern. "Did I hurt you? I saw you about to fall into the pool and reacted without thinking. I didn't mean to make us fall like that."

"No, no, I'm fine," I assured him. "Thank you so much for catching me. It's too cold for a swim."

"For sure." That smile was tentatively returning.

"I just bumped my nose on your ridiculously hard chest when we landed, that's all."

He cringed. "Does it hurt?"

"Nah, it's fine." I prodded it just to double-check. It had hurt only on impact. "What's under that T-shirt anyway? You got a bulletproof vest under there or something?"

Mason stood a bit taller, puffing his chest out a tiny bit. When he reached up and tugged on the collar of his T-shirt, my gaze dipped to the bit of exposed skin on display. I had the urge to run my fingers over the dusting of hair covering that very firm chest.

"No Kevlar," he said, releasing the fabric and making me snap my eyes up. "It's just a side effect of my job. I work in construction, and I end up doing a lot of the heavy lifting."

"Why do you get stuck with all the grunt work?"

"To be fair, it's one of the reasons I was hired. I have super strength. It's cheaper to pay me a Variant surcharge than it is to hire equipment on most jobs."

"Right. Of course." I nodded. I had no idea that "Variant surcharge" was even a thing, but then I didn't grow up around a lot of working-class people. I was aware of my privileged upbringing, but moments like this really drove the point home. "So, you have a Vital? Is she here some-where? Or he?"

I glanced around the yard, searching for someone who looked as if they might be with Mason.

He shook his head, looking amused.

"So, how do you know Kid?" I asked, just as the guy in question started showing off his own Variant ability. He was drawing balls of flame from the firepit and throwing them into the air while a bunch of people around him played chicken with the fire hurtling down. It always fizzled to nothing before it came near anyone's head.

"I don't." Mason shrugged. "Not really. My cousin is a football buddy of his. He invited me along because I happened to be in town visiting family. I live in Brooklyn and mostly work in Manhattan. How about you?"

"Oh, I'm a student at Bradford Hills Institute. I've known most of these dickheads since childhood." I chuckled. "I'm in my final year and a half now," I hastened to add, not wanting him to think I was too young.

Too young for what? You have a boyfriend! Who might just be your Bonded Variant.

"Oriana!" Dot came jogging up. "Someone said you nearly ended up in the pool. You good?"

"Yeah, fine, thanks to Mason here!"

I did the introductions, and then Mason's cousin joined us as well. I knew him—we'd been in some of the same Variant studies classes a few years ago—but not well. A few others wandered over, and we all settled on the grass to chat.

Except Mason and I kept breaking off, drawing each other into deeper side conversations, our heads bent.

I told him about studying business and design, and my grand shoe brand plans for after graduation. He told me a little about his job and his family in the city. We cracked jokes and, by the time the party was winding down, were teasing each other as though we'd known each other all our lives and not just a few short hours.

In an unusual lull in the conversation, I couldn't hold back a yawn. When I pried my eyes open, I realized most of the party people had cleared out and Mason and I were sitting alone on the lawn . . . unless you counted the couple making out in the shallow end of the pool.

"I'd better get to bed," I said, reluctantly pushing to my feet. I grabbed my phone and bugged my eyes out when I saw the time. I hadn't planned on staying this late—or early. A quick check of the group chat told me Crystal and Ebony had both left hours ago. Ebony was staying with Derek, and Crystal hadn't specified.

"Yeah, me too." Mason brushed loose grass off his butt and grabbed his own phone. "I better find my . . . er . . . or not. Looks like my cousin took some girl home and I'm stuck walking back to my aunt and uncle's."

"Guess we're both walking."

We didn't agree to walk together, nor did we ask the other where we were heading, but we kept chatting as we strolled off. I ditched my heels at the end of the gravel driveway, thankful that campus was only a short walk away.

As we rounded the corner onto a street near my res hall, we slowed, staring at the scene before us.

Flashing lights made me squint against the brightness. Several police cars and an ambulance surrounded what looked like the scene of an accident.

"Holy shit," I breathed as we slowly walked forward. I wasn't sure whether I wanted to watch to find out what was happening, or tuck my face into Mason's shoulder and hurry to the campus gate.

"They need help." Mason rushed toward the scene, taking the decision out of my hands, and I jogged after him. There was a pickup off to the side, its front mangled, but that wasn't the site of all the buzzing activity. The other car involved was a sedan now plastered around a pole. It looked as if the pickup had rammed into its side and pinned it against the pole before backing off.

"Sir, you need to back up," an officer at the edge of the scene barked at Mason.

Mason stopped immediately and held his hands up. "I

have an enhanced strength ability. They look like they're struggling to get that door open. I'm just offering my help."

The officer glanced between Mason and the several people trying to pry the car open with crowbars, his expression uncertain. Then he nodded and motioned for Mason to follow.

I stayed out of the way as I put my shoes back on, worried about glass on the ground.

After a hurried back-and-forth with the officers, someone handed Mason a pair of gloves, and he positioned himself in front of the passenger door. He would pull on it while two others used crowbars to put pressure on the other side.

It took a few tries and some readjustments of grip and angle, but then a creaking of metal rent the night air. I gasped, transfixed, as Mason literally pried apart twisted metal with his bare hands.

Super strength may have been one of the more common Variant abilities, but anyone who thought it was boring was an idiot.

Mason stumbled back as the door finally released. Waiting paramedics rushed forward, and I gasped again as they started to pull a heavily pregnant woman out of the car.

The paramedics and police had their hands full with the pregnant woman, the unconscious driver, and the hysterical driver of the pickup. After a hasty pat on the back and a handshake, no one paid Mason any attention, and he slowly made his way over to me.

"Oh my god, Mason! That was amazing!" I gushed.

"Eh. All in a day's work, Oreo." He waved his hand dismissively, his words slurred. *Did he just call me Oreo?* Up close, I could see his eyes drooping slightly, the way his feet dragged on the ground.

He'd been a bit tipsy from the party, but not stumbling and slurring. We'd been having a conversation as we walked.

Something was wrong with Mason, and I had a feeling I knew what it was.

FOUR

Unease churned in my gut as we made our way through the grounds of BHI. I was comforted by the fact he could still walk, but any Variant or Vital would know he might be in serious trouble.

Mason stumbled slightly over his own feet, and my worry for him doubled.

He'd pushed his ability past its limits. He didn't look as if he was in pain, but something deep inside me knew that something deep inside him was suffering. He'd used up way too much of the limited Light he had access to, and his physical body was paying for it.

"We need to get you somewhere warm." I gripped his arm to steady him, hoping he could get up the stairs to my room. My res hall was close.

"I'm OK. I just need to . . ." He trailed off, his voice weak and low.

"You're *not* OK." I stopped and faced him, sliding my hand down his arm. He needed Light and I had it—it was practically writhing against my skin to come out. I took his hand in mine.

The Light came pouring out of me and into him, gushing through the one point of contact.

Mason grunted and took an unsteady step closer, releasing a shuddering breath as he gripped my waist. His hold was gentle, weak; both his hands felt as if they grasped on to me with all the remaining strength he had.

I placed my free hand on the side of his neck, giving the Light another point of contact to transfer. The extra Light made Mason whimper; his hold on me strengthened as he stumbled backward. We didn't go far. His back connected with a thick oak trunk, and for the second time that night, I found myself falling into him.

Was it because he was so depleted that the Light flowed to him this easily? Any other time I transferred Light to someone, I had to focus. It took effort to draw it into myself and even more effort to push it into a Variant.

Transferring Light to Mason took no effort or focus whatsoever. The Light just flowed as though it knew exactly what it needed to do. It was as effortless as breathing, as easy as when I transferred to Leon. Easier even . . .

Mine.

My Light had known it before I did, but Mason was mine. I could've rationalized it away as extreme circumstances. Maybe if Mason hadn't been so depleted, I might've done just that—reasoned it away until I spoke to Leon, until the Light made it impossible for me to stay away from Mason.

But I was running on pure instinct.

He was hurting and he needed me and he was *mine.*

"Holy . . . shit . . . ," Mason panted, his eyes wide as he stared at me.

I didn't reply. I just shoved his jacket off his shoulders

and ran my hands up his arms, craving as much skin-on-skin contact as I could get.

His hands went to my back. He shivered, and his fingers tangled with the crisscrossing fabric of my strappy dress to find more skin.

The Light was bursting at my seams. He needed *more* and I needed *him*.

We leaned in at the same time, like a perfectly choreographed dance practiced for countless hours. Our lips crashed together, and he moaned into my mouth. My tongue tingled where it swiped against his. My lips tingled where they met his. Every part of my body that touched his —that let the Light flow between us—tingled pleasantly.

"We should . . . ," Mason panted.

"Yeah . . . ," I breathed, running my tongue up his neck.

"Need you," he groaned, rolling his hips, his body telling me exactly what he needed.

"Yes." I hitched a leg over his hip and ground against his erection. His fingers dug into my thigh, some strength returning to his grip.

"I want . . . but not . . ." Frustration and lust laced his words as he struggled to speak between messy, desperate kisses.

"Not out here," I managed to rush out, finishing his sentence.

My Light was reviving him; he was clearly mine—not a sliver of doubt remained in my mind—and I needed to feel him, give him all the Light I had until the undeniable connection between us was satisfied.

"This way." I managed to pull away, the Light straining against my skin in protest. Keeping contact, I pulled Mason in the direction of my res hall. He was just as desperate to remain glued to me, his hands running over my body as we stumbled up the stairs to the front door.

We were a panting, groping, stumbling mess of desperation as we made our way through the building and to my room. The living area was dark as I kicked the door closed behind us, my lips fused to his.

I kept moving us toward my room as I fumbled with the buttons on his shirt. With an impatient huff, Mason shoved my hands out of the way and yanked the two halves apart, sending buttons clattering all around the room.

His shirt lay forgotten on the floor, along with our shoes and my bag. Now that we were no longer out in the open, any last inhibitions I may have had completely melted away. It didn't matter that we'd met only a few hours earlier, that I had a boyfriend, that we hadn't even acknowledged we were Bonded.

All that mattered was that I was his Vital, he was my Variant, and the Light was demanding we come together with as much skin contact as possible. I'd never craved someone's body as I did that night. I felt as if I might die if I were forced to leave Mason's embrace, as if I wouldn't be able to function without him next to me, inside me.

I tugged on the bow at the small of my back, loosening the straps of my dress, and Mason yanked it off my shoulders. I shoved his pants and underwear down in one go as I stepped out of my dress, nudging him toward my bed.

We fell onto the mattress, my messy, unmade sheets tangling even more under our writhing bodies. I slid my underwear down my legs, and we were finally, blissfully, fully naked. We were chest to chest, kissing deeply, our legs hooked around each other, our hands caressing, clawing, worshipping this intense connection we shared.

I can't even remember if I was on my back or straddling

him or if we were on our sides as he slid into my aching, dripping core. All I remember is the sense of rightness as he filled me, the delicious stretch of him, the intense pleasure of feeling him inside me.

We started moving as one, our hips thrusting in sharp, desperate movements. The room filled with the sounds of our joining—skin slapping against wet skin, moans and groans and even sobs as we fully surrendered to our connection.

It couldn't have been more than a few minutes before an orgasm coursed through me. It felt as though every inch of my body tingled and ached as I shattered into a million pieces and was put back together by the man between my legs—all in the space of a few seconds.

Mason came at the same time, grinding his hips against me and groaning, as though trying to get even deeper inside me.

Panting, sweaty, sticky, we fell asleep in each other's arms.

FIVE

Mason and I spent the remaining hours before dawn having sex and napping in between. I couldn't get enough of him, and the feeling was clearly mutual, judging by how quickly he got hard for me over and over again. It felt like a fever dream of sex and Light and that hazy space between sleep and waking where anything seemed possible.

We eventually fell asleep for a longer stretch, and reality came crashing down when I woke up properly, late the next morning.

I couldn't believe I'd finally found my Bonded Variant. I watched Mason's peaceful face, his lips barely parted as he slept wrapped around me. In the bright morning light, I could see bits of red streaked through his otherwise dark hair. My heart was so full, and a soft smile pulled at my lips.

But guilt swiftly followed the happiness, shattering the brief moment of contentment.

Leon.

It didn't feel right crying over Leon while I was still in Mason's arms, so I slowly sat up, doing my best to keep my tears silent until I could make it to the bathroom. But I didn't even make it out of my bed.

"Oriana?" Mason's voice was rough from sleep. He sat up behind me as I swung my legs off the side of the bed, and caressed my bare shoulder. "What's wrong?"

I shook my head, dropping my face into my hands and sobbing. Mason cursed under his breath and shuffled to sit next to me.

"Did I hurt you?" He sounded a bit panicky. I couldn't blame him. Crying hysterically after hooking up with someone was bad form, but it couldn't be helped. "Oh god, I'm so sorry. Everything is a bit of a blur after the—"

"You didn't hurt me," I sniffled, finally looking into his eyes. Instantly I felt calmer. He was my Variant, and he was holding me and caring for me and everything would be OK.

"I can't stand to see you upset." He looked physically pained. "Especially now that I know you're my Vital."

"I know. It's not you, I promise. I can't tell you how happy I am that we found each other." Another round of messy sobs contradicted the sentiment.

Mason just held me and waited until I could speak.

I forced myself to look at him as I said it. "Mason, I have a boyfriend, remember?"

"Oh." His hands stopped moving up and down my arms, but he seemed reluctant or unable to drop them. He looked crushed, and I rushed to explain.

"I want to be with you, obviously. We're Bonded. I'm excited about this, *us*. But I really like . . . *liked* him. And breaking up with him is going to be hard." I hated myself a little for putting that hurt feeling in his eyes, for the hurt I knew I'd be causing Leon. I'd thought Leon was mine, but the way my Light had *gushed* out of me to Mason last night —nothing could compare to that.

Mason pulled me in for a tight hug, not saying anything. What was there to say? It was a shitty situation, but the sooner I dealt with it the sooner we could all start to heal.

Mason and I spent the rest of the day hanging out, mostly in my room. We didn't have sex. It just didn't feel right until the situation with Leon was resolved. When we remembered we'd had unprotected sex in our Light-fueled frenzy, we had that awkward talk. Neither of us had hooked up with anyone without a condom, so we weren't worried about STDs, and I reassured him I had the implant. He may have been my Bonded Variant, but neither of us was anywhere near ready for kids.

He had to head back to Brooklyn in the afternoon so he could go to work the next day.

I spent the evening, most of the sleepless night, and a distracted morning of classes anxious about seeing Leon. His flight landed in the afternoon, and we organized to meet up at a café on campus. It was close to where my last lecture for the day was, and he'd make it there just as I finished. I didn't want to put this off for a second.

He stood from his chair at an outdoor table as I approached, his brow furrowed in worry. I'd avoided any calls and kept our messages to a minimum. I gave him a weak smile as I reached his side, intending to just sit down, but his frown deepened, and he pulled me into a hug before I could stop him.

Despite knowing I shouldn't, I melted into him, my arms going around his waist. His leather-and-tangerine smell wrapped around me, and I breathed him in. Why was life being so cruel to us both?

"God, I missed you." He kissed the top of my head.

"I missed you too," I whispered against his shoulder as my eyes started to water.

Leon pulled back to look into my face. "Oriana, what's going on? I feel like you're about to tell me something horrible."

I forced myself to step back, and we sat at the little table. Through barely restrained tears, I told him everything. All his emotions were written on his beautiful face as he listened, his body shrinking in on itself. I hated every second of it.

"I'm so sorry, Leon," I finished lamely but honestly. "I hope you know I wouldn't be doing this if he wasn't my Variant."

We both knew any kind of relationship was impossible outside of my Bond. Leon stared at the table between us, his hands hanging between his legs. After a while, he shook his head, sat up straight, and looked up to meet my gaze.

"No." He frowned.

"What do you mean *no*?" I hated doing this so much. I was falling in love with Leon, but I couldn't be with him when he wasn't my Bonded. "Leon, he's my Variant. I know it in my soul."

"I don't doubt it, Oriana. If your Light is telling you he's yours, then he is. But I refuse to accept that this is the end for us. I'm yours too."

A little bit of hope flared in my chest. I did have a very strong connection to Leon; I was drawn to him. Breaking up with him felt like breaking off a piece of myself. Maybe he was mine too. But . . .

"You have no idea how much I wish that was true." My voice broke on the last word as tears blurred my vision. I had to clear my throat. "But the way my Light came gushing out for him . . . It was effortless with you, but it was on a whole other level with him."

He winced at that, and I felt as though I was stabbing us both in the gut, a blade in each hand as I twisted.

"But he'd used his ability, right?" There was something a little frantic in Leon's eyes. "You said that—he'd pushed himself way past his limit. That's why the Light gushed so intensely. That doesn't mean it won't do the same for me."

"There's no way to know that, and don't you dare put yourself in danger to prove a point." I wagged a finger at him, worried he'd do just that.

"I won't, I won't," he reassured me, stepping closer and rubbing my shoulders. His touch was so soothing, so comforting. I wanted to cry. But I knew I couldn't lean into it as much as I wanted to.

"Leon . . . ," I sniffled as the torment tracked down my cheeks.

"I'll prove it to you another way." He squeezed my shoulders, and I wiped at my eyes with my shirtsleeve, frowning at him.

"How?"

"Hit me." He smiled as if this was the best idea he'd ever had.

"What?" I sobbed. This was going so much worse than I'd even imagined.

"A Variant's ability, no matter how destructive, is harmless to their Vital."

I nodded. Everyone knew this.

"You've transferred Light to me before. We may not have completed the Bond, solidified it, but your Light will recognize me as yours. Or it won't . . . and we'll know either way."

"I'm not even sure how your ability works?" I raised my voice a little, frustration adding to the shit-pile of emotions inside me.

Leon grabbed my hand and pulled me over to a group of students hanging out near the entrance to the coffee shop. "Hey, guys, can you help me prove a point to my girl?"

The two guys and one chick all looked at me uncertainly, then the girl clocked Leon's hand wrapped around mine and narrowed her gaze. I was still crying; Leon was a little crazed in his determination—I would've jumped to conclusions too.

"Hey, man." One of the dudes slowly stepped closer. "Why don't you just let the lady go and we can talk about this."

"Huh?" Leon looked so confused for a second it almost made me laugh. But he quickly dropped my hand. "Oh shit! Nah, it's nothing like that. Look, can one of you just punch me so I can show her how my ability works?"

The guys shared disturbed looks, and the girl addressed me directly. "Want me to call campus security?"

I shook my head immediately. Not for a second did I worry Leon might hurt me or do something to put me in danger. "No. I'm fine, really." I sighed and turned to the guys. "Just hit him."

The guy standing closest to us shrugged and punched Leon in the left shoulder. It didn't look as if he put his full force behind it, but it didn't look light either. It made Leon flinch and rub the spot—and the guy who punched him released a surprised yelp of pain, rubbing the same spot on his own left shoulder.

"What the fuck?" He took a step back, eyeing Leon warily.

"Thanks, man!" Leon waved at him and put his full focus on me. "See? Reverberation. He hit me, and he felt it just as much as I did. But you'll hit me, and you won't feel anything because you're my Vital. I just know it."

"I'm not going to hit you, Leon."

"Then pinch me or something."

"No!"

"Yes! Just do it!"

"I'm in enough pain already today!"

"It. Won't. Hurt. You!"

"Argh! You are such a jerk!"

"I know! Doesn't that make you want to slap me?"

You know what? I raised my hand and swung it at his face, slapping him right across his cheek.

I gasped and balled my hands into fists under my chin. He was acting crazy and this was such an emotionally charged day and he just wouldn't let up, so I'd acted on that final straw of frustration and gave him what he was asking for.

And *immediately* regretted it. I was breaking up with the guy and he was not taking it well, and to top it all off, I had to go and slap him too. A fresh wave of tears tracked down my cheeks.

"Oh my god, Leon! I'm so sorry!"

"Does it hurt?" he asked, rubbing his cheek. It was already turning pink.

"Huh?" I frowned and touched my own cheek with the tips of my fingers.

"You smacked me good, baby. Does your cheek hurt too?"

I blinked and made myself actually pay attention to my body. My palm stung and my chest felt as though it was caving in, but my cheek was fine.

My eyes widened as I stared at Leon. Now that I was actually tuned in to my body, I could feel the Light inside me straining to get to him. There was a reason his touch felt comforting, a reason I felt so much more grounded when I saw him, a reason why it felt so wrong to break up with him.

There was a reason why my cheek didn't sting one bit.

Leon was mine. He was my Bonded Variant, and I was his Vital. He was as much mine as Mason was.

"It doesn't hurt at all," I sobbed.

I caught only a brief glimpse of his grin before I launched myself into his arms and buried my face in his neck. He caught me easily, gripping my thighs as I wrapped my legs around him. That subtle tangerine scent soothed all the jagged, inflamed parts of my insides that had been tearing apart.

He was mine. I didn't have to lose him.

He held me tightly, as though he was scared if he let go, I might disappear. I couldn't blame him.

A small round of applause erupted around us. The group of students we'd approached had been joined by a few more, and they'd all witnessed our dramatic revelation that we were Bonded.

"Glad it worked out for you, girl!" the chick that had been ready to protect me called out.

"This is so beautiful." The guy who'd punched Leon sounded choked up, and his friends laughed at him as they all dispersed.

Leon set me back down on my feet, but we remained in each other's arms. Neither of us wanted to be apart, so when he asked me to come home with him, I readily agreed. We held hands the whole way as Leon drove to his apartment nearby, as we made our way upstairs, and even as he fumbled one-handed to unlock the door.

"I need to grab a shower," he said, wheeling his suitcase into a corner. "Then we could get some takeout. Or would you prefer to go out? Somewhere nice to celebrate, maybe?"

I scrunched my nose up at the idea as I wrapped my arms around his neck. "Stay in. I want you all to myself."

"You've got me, baby. I'm not going anywhere." His earnest declaration melted me, and the tender kiss he followed it up with had me clinging to him tighter.

Eventually, he pulled away and told me to make myself at home, then headed to the bathroom. As the shower started up, I called Mason to update him.

"Wow. Really? That's . . . uh . . . yeah. Wow." He was clearly surprised by my news, but I wasn't sure if he was upset.

"Are you OK? I hope you're not mad." I chewed on my bottom lip.

"Mad? No!" He laughed. "I'm not mad at all, Oreo. I'm just surprised. I never even expected to have a Vital. This is all kind of new to me."

I released an audible breath of relief. "Good. OK."

"Yeah. One step at a time. I look forward to meeting him."

"Man, the past few days have been a roller coaster."

"I can imagine. I wish so badly I could give you a hug right now." The longing in his voice was palpable.

"Me too." I glanced at the bathroom door.

"Go get a cuddle from your other boyfriend for me." Mason chuckled, reading my mind, and we ended the call.

The shower was still running, but I made my way to the door anyway. Leon and I had been taking the physical stuff slowly, getting to know each other, skirting the question of whether we were Bonded or not. But now I knew he was mine, and after nearly losing him at my own hand, I needed more.

I knocked softly and opened the door inch by inch, giving him plenty of time to tell me to get the fuck out.

"Oriana?" he called from behind the steamed-up glass of the shower.

"Got room for one more?" I asked.

His head appeared around the side of the glass, and *god*, he was beautiful. He always looked devastatingly handsome, but there was something arresting about seeing him with his hair plastered to his scalp and water droplets all over his face.

In answer to my nervous question, he just smiled and held out a wet arm in invitation.

I undressed, resisting the urge to cover myself. It was only a momentary pang of insecurity. The Light-driven connection between us was a much stronger force, and it drove me to bare all to my Bonded—in more ways than one.

Taking his hand, I stepped into the shower, and Leon wrapped his arms around me as he drew me under the spray. The water was hot, but the man pressing every inch of his wet, naked, sculpted body against mine was hotter.

We kissed languidly, unhurriedly, as our hands explored. I caressed the dips and smooth surfaces of his strong shoulders, back, chest, ass—anywhere I could reach. He did the same, his hands roaming my body, his touch gentle and teasing here, possessive and firm there.

He grew hard between us, and I couldn't resist reaching down to wrap my hand around him. I pumped him slowly, teasing, as he dragged a hand down my front. His fingers caressed from my throat all the way down to between my legs.

The Light flowed freely between us, the sensation intensifying the pleasure we gave each other as the water beat down on our shoulders. I had suspected the Light was the extra element making my previous encounters with Leon that much more intense. Now that I knew for sure—

43

now that I'd experienced the undeniable force with which it brought me and Mason together—it seemed so obvious.

It had been intense and desperate with Mason. There was no element of danger with Leon though, so when we finally came together, I could feel the Light *sing* at the joining of two souls bound by it.

Leon moved us so my back pressed against the tiles, and I lifted a leg to wrap around his hip.

"Fuck," he muttered, forcing himself to pull back and look at me. "Condom?"

I shook my head. "Implant. I'm clean."

"Me too."

The words hadn't even fully left his mouth before I pulled him back in for a kiss. He angled his hips just so and slid into me inch by inch.

We took our time, moving slowly at first, exploring what we liked, at times just holding still while I felt him deep inside me and we breathed the same humid air. We found a rhythm eventually, and with an extra few fingers working my clit, we reached the peak together.

It was a drawn-out, full-body orgasm that seemed to go on for both eons and barely a nanosecond. Our shared pleasure echoed off the tiles along with our moans.

Absolutely exhausted from everything that had happened over the past few days, I let Leon carry me to his bed after. I smiled against his bare shoulder, feeling as if everything had clicked into place at last.

SIX

Leon's steady grip on my hand felt like the only thing keeping me from bouncing into the air. I was about ready to burst from excitement.

Leon smiled down at me, amusement lighting up his gaze. The crossing light was still red, that little crimson man and a few feet of pavement the only thing between me and Mason.

I hadn't seen him since the night we met, he overused his ability, and we Bonded. The hour drive, coupled with his work schedule and my study workload, had kept us apart for two whole weeks. We spoke on the phone every day and texted all the time, but I missed him so much it hurt.

The light finally changed, and I took off, pulling Leon behind me. Leon had been amazing since we realized we were Bonded too. He was around all the time and taking all the extra Light I had coursing through me, driving me to Mason.

They were finally going to meet for the first time.

A slight drizzle dampened my head and shoulders as we made our way toward the restaurant, but nothing was going to dampen my mood. I was about to have my Bond together, complete at last.

I spotted Mason before he saw us. He was seated at a table in the alfresco area, under the canopy of leafy trees, his leg bouncing.

He turned his head and spotted me, and his whole face lit up with a grin. The chair scraped on the pavers as he shot to his feet and rushed toward me. I dropped Leon's hand and ran into Mason's arms.

When I wrapped my arms around his neck, he spun me on the spot. My head was already spinning from how happy and excited I was anyway, so it just gave me an excuse to let loose my giggle. His lips were on mine before my feet settled back on the ground, but he had the presence of mind to keep it PG. Everything had fallen away for me—I was only aware of his touch, his smell, his lips on mine, and Leon's presence a few feet behind us—but Mason clearly remembered we were in the middle of Manhattan on a Saturday and there were people everywhere.

He pressed his forehead to mine and caressed my cheek with one thumb.

"I missed you so much," I whispered against his lips.

"I've never missed someone so much in my life." He gave me one more soft kiss and pulled back to smile at me. "Now introduce me to your other Variant."

We turned as one to face Leon and . . .

Mason's entire body stiffened. The arm he still had around my waist turned to a steel pole, his body a brick wall.

Leon looked just as stiff. He was frowning, his jaw hard, his hands in fists at his sides.

My smile faltered, some of their tension infusing my own body and gathering deep in my chest.

"Oriana," Leon gritted out. He turned his glare from

Mason to me, his eyes only softening a fraction. "Please tell me this isn't the guy you fused to our Bond."

"What?" Who else would I be running up to and kissing like that? I thought they were both fine with having another Variant in the Bond. What the hell was happening? "Leon, this is . . ."

"Mason Shaw," Leon barked. I flinched slightly at the venom in his tone.

"Your other Variant is Leon Livingston?" Mason's voice was flat, emotionless, as impassive as the brick wall his body felt like. He dropped his arm from around me, and that ball of tension in my chest dropped heavily into my gut.

I turned what I was sure was a wide-eyed, desperate look toward Mason. His face was as flat as his voice, his shoulders tight, and his eyes? His eyes bored into mine, full of *betrayal*.

"Mason, I . . . Leon . . ." I looked between my two Bonded Variants, lost for words. "What's happening?"

"Is this some kind of sick fucking joke?" Leon stepped closer to Mason, who squared up, eyes blazing.

"Only you would think me finding my Vital was about *you*," Mason spat.

"She's *my* Vital. I met her first."

"So? I Bonded with her first."

"Yeah? And I've been *bonding* with her every day since."

"Yet she still couldn't wait to run into *my* arms."

My gaze whipped from side to side as they argued like mortal enemies. Over me. They were tearing me apart, straight down the middle. This was supposed to be a wonderful day—when my life would feel complete.

How the fuck was it going this wrong?

My breathing became ragged as I wrung my hands. I

was at a complete loss as to what to do or say. The Light inside me felt as if it was sparking, stinging with every harsh word my two Bonded Variants volleyed at each other. It wanted me to soothe the connection, settle the Bond.

But I was breaking, and I didn't know where to begin mending any of this.

Mason and Leon continued to bicker, but I lost track of what they actually said. Everything became muffled beneath the sudden ringing in my ears. Needing some room to breathe, I took an unsteady step back, and they both whipped their heads around to look at me.

They wore matching angry, mean expressions. Having the leftover vitriol aimed in my direction felt like a punch to the gut, and I stumbled back another step.

Both my Variants moved toward me, arms outstretched. Then they realized their unintended synchronicity and turned vicious glares back on each other.

Leon growled through gritted teeth and turned away. Without so much as a glance at me, he stalked up the street and disappeared around a corner.

Mason paced back and forth with his hands on his hips until the fight drained out of him. With one long exhale, he sank back into his seat and dropped his head into his hands.

I looked in the direction of where Leon had disappeared, then back at Mason, who looked completely defeated. I had no idea where Leon was going or how far his agitated steps would take him, but Mason felt just as distant, despite the fact he was sitting right in front of me.

The drizzly clouds floated away to make room for the sun high above the trees. It was turning into a beautiful day, but nothing could penetrate the darkness that had settled over me.

SEVEN

I stood on Ebony's right, staring at the couch in our shared living area. On her other side, Crystal hummed and cocked her head.

"Maybe it would be better under the window," she mused.

All three of us turned to look at the area under the window. Our room faced the back of the building, so that window had a view of the grounds of Bradford Hills Institute. We wanted to make the best of the view, so all the furniture in the limited space had been moved multiple times over the past fifteen minutes.

Mason picked up the heavy three-seater as if it were a wicker chair and placed it under the window.

"How's that?" He grinned. The three of us regarded the piece of furniture in its third potential location.

Having someone with super strength to help with this process was really handy. Not that we'd planned to move the room around. Mason had come over, and my roomies had roped him into helping not even a few minutes after I made the introductions. He was happy to do it and seemed pleased to be making a good first impression.

Just the day before, he'd moved into his aunt and uncle's house in downtown Bradford Hills. They'd helped him find a job in the area and were letting him stay in their basement until he found a more permanent solution.

One of the things Mason had been looking forward to telling me on that disastrous day was that he'd quit the job in Manhattan and made plans to move closer to me. Not that we got to discuss it properly, or at all. Leon came back not long after leaving, having cooled down, and we had a tense, silent drive back to Bradford Hills.

Mason told me about his plans on the phone the day after. It had been two weeks since then, and I was still no closer to finding out the cause of this catastrophic rift between them.

I'd reassured him that I didn't want him to feel obligated to move for me, but he brushed it off. He could find work anywhere, and he wanted to be close to me. It was hard for Bonds to be apart, especially during the early stages. Plus, with him in Bradford Hills, we could take advantage of the mentoring and training BHI offered to students with new Bonds.

The help with managing enhanced powers and learning how to control my Light would've been really useful, but I was reluctant to start the training with my Variants still not speaking to each other. I had put off telling my family my exciting news for the same reason.

"I think this is the spot," I declared, plonking down in the middle of the couch.

"You don't think it blocks the view?" Ebony frowned.

"Hardly." I shrugged and twisted to look through the window. The couch was barely a few inches taller than the window ledge. It was a beautiful day out there, and I looked forward to showing Mason around the campus.

"It's too awkward anywhere else," Crystal sighed, and it was decided. We fussed with the rest of the furniture, rearranging it so the TV and the armchair and the makeshift kitchen were all set up just so. Mason chatted with my friends, and I loved that they got along. They seemed to really like him. They liked Leon too. If only my Bonded Variants could figure their shit out . . .

As I suggested to Mason that we get going, someone knocked on the door.

Ebony was the closest and got up to answer it.

Leon breezed into the room.

He spotted me and Mason right away, and his relaxed smile fell. I hated how fast his expression shuttered, his eyes going cold. I hated how Mason tensed as his arms dropped from around me.

I hated everything about this.

It had been two weeks of them avoiding each other, avoiding any mentions of the fact that I had two Bonded Variants, avoiding my questions about what their issues were. It would be impossible for them to ignore each other now that Mason had moved here.

"What are you doing here?" Leon asked, sounding deeply inconvenienced.

"Unlike you, I was actually invited," Mason replied, his voice sarcastically polite. "What are *you* doing here?"

"I'm here to see my Vital. You got a problem with that?"

"Yeah, I do, asshole. I've got a problem with breathing the same air as her."

"The thought of your dirty hands on her makes me sick."

"My dirty hands? What the fuck is that supposed to

mean, you spoiled man-child brat?"

"Enough!" I yelled, stomping my foot for good measure. My two problem Variants and my two roomies all turned surprised expressions my way.

It took a lot to make me truly angry, and I never shouted. But they were making me feel like a tug toy clutched in the jaws of two growling dogs, being torn apart.

"I can't do this." I forced a measured tone into my firm words. "You refuse to talk about what your problems are, but you refuse to acknowledge that this bullshit is affecting me. I'm right here—in the damn middle—and I can't keep feeling like this every time you're even mentioned in the same sentence, let alone in the same room. I . . ." The tightness in my throat made it impossible to keep speaking. I looked up to the ceiling and took a breath. I refused to cry.

"Baby, don't cry. I'm sorry," Leon pleaded.

"I'm sorry, Oreo," Mason said at the same moment.

I looked at them just in time to see both their jaws clench at being spoken over. They had more in common than they thought. Or maybe they knew how much they had in common. What the hell did I know? They wouldn't tell me anything.

"I accept that neither of you wants to hurt me, not on purpose. But now that Mason has moved here"—Leon turned a quick irritated look at Mason, but I forged on —"shit like this is going to keep happening. So, what can we do to fix it?"

I wasn't going to try to solve a problem I didn't even know the extent of, but I needed them to pull their heads out of their asses and start doing something about this.

"How about . . ." Leon looked off to the side, thinking, as Mason sighed and crossed his arms. "How about a calendar?"

Mason and I both frowned, but Leon explained his brilliant idea, smiling as though he was really onto something. "We can create a joint calendar that we all have access to. That way we'll know when one of us is spending time with Oriana, and the other can stay away."

"Organize dates and times to do shit together that works with our schedules." Mason rubbed his chin. "Yeah, this could work."

I gaped at them. Were they serious? I caught a glimpse of my roomies, sitting together on the couch, watching this trainwreck unfold. Ebony was rubbing her forehead, while Crystal had a permanent expression of cringe on her face.

"Get out," I barked, pointing to the door.

My Variants looked at me, genuinely surprised, then shared a frown.

"Me?" Leon pressed a hand to his chest. "I know Mason was here first but—"

"Out!" I was shouting again. "Both of you—get the fuck out of my sight immediately."

"Oriana?" Mason dared to take a step closer, reaching out as if to soothe me.

I stepped out of his reach and held both hands out to keep the two men away from me. "Are you listening to yourselves? The first thing you've agreed on is a more organized way to avoid each other. That's seriously your solution? A fucking custody agreement? I am not a kid in your messy divorce, nor am I a time-share in Florida. I am your Vital. Now get the hell out before I say something I don't mean."

Tugging at his hair, Mason stomped to the door and disappeared in a huff. After another second of hesitation, Leon followed him out with a sigh.

Crystal got up and closed the door, then turned both locks decisively.

EIGHT

I was always starving by the end of Business Ethics on Tuesday. The class started right after another lecture and ended at 1:30 p.m., leaving me no time to have lunch until after.

So I was extra irritable when I walked out to find Leon standing near the building's entrance, a dozen red roses clutched in his hand.

He looked handsome in his blue linen suit, his hair neatly styled, his smile hesitant. Rolling my eyes, I tried to walk past him, but he stepped into my path. I could probably have managed to walk away if I'd tried hard enough, but I was weak from lack of sustenance, and the Light was pushing against my skin, desperate to get to my Bonded.

"Oriana, please," he rushed out, holding the fragrant flowers out to me. "I'm sorry. I miss you. I just want to talk."

Reflexively, I took the flowers from him. "Are you ready to talk about why you hate Mason so much?"

He pressed his lips into a thin line and sighed. That was all the answer I needed.

"Then we have nothing to talk about." It physically hurt

to have him *right there* and not feel his skin on mine, not let the Light course between us, but I marched past him and dumped the roses in the nearest trash can without skipping a single step.

It had been only a few days since I threw them both out of my res hall, but the apologetic texts had started up that same day. Then the calls and gifts—a jewelry box from Leon on my doorstep, my favorite macaroons from Mason delivered all the way from Manhattan. Apparently, we were now moving on to stage three of the groveling—in-person ambush.

They were both blowing up my phone with calls and texts, but I'd made it clear I wasn't going to speak to them until they figured out their issues and/or told me why they hated each other so much. They weren't talking, so I wasn't opening the gifts or replying to their messages.

I speed-walked to the dining hall and moped through lunch, sitting in a corner by myself and eating my weight in spaghetti.

The next morning—my only morning to sleep in, since I had no classes until after lunch—I was woken at seven by a knock at the door. The girls had classes, so I stumbled out of bed with a groan and shuffled to answer the door.

A barber-shop quartet stood on the other side, with red-and-white-striped vests and those straw hats and everything. They took a collective deep breath, ready to burst into song. I slammed the door closed in their faces.

After a split second, I opened it again. "Nothing personal, guys. I'm just in a fight with my boyfriend and don't want to hear it." They cringed and shared uncertain looks. "Which one of them thought this was a good idea?"

One of the singers cleared his throat and handed over a small card. "Mason Shaw," he said as I read it.

Without further ado, they turned and headed toward the elevator. As they cleared out, a delivery chick stepped up to the door, and I groaned.

"Yeah, hi." She blew a bubble with her chewing gum. "I have a feeling you're not going to want this one either, but . . ." She held out a flat black box with my name on it and a screen to sign for the delivery.

I signed, sent her on her way, and slammed my door shut.

Trying to go back to sleep was pointless, so I got dressed and took myself out for breakfast. My fave café did the best pancakes and excellent lattes, but even that couldn't fully lift my mood.

On my way back, I decided to take a longer way. It was a nice sunny day, and the path took me past a wooded area. Maybe my Light was working on some subconscious or supernatural level, because the path also took me right past the construction site for a house. Where Mason was currently working.

Half the crew had their shirts off as they buzzed around drilling and sawing and hammering things. I had eyes only for Mason. The tattoo on his back was mesmerizing, even from a distance. His strong, lean body moved fluidly as he alternated between cutting pieces of wood and lifting them up to some guys on scaffolding, as if the wooden beams weighed nothing.

It didn't take long for him to spot me. I was just standing at the bottom of what would be the driveway when they finished building. He said something to a guy standing nearby and jogged over.

"Oriana. Hey." His grin was as brilliant as the sun as he leaned in for a kiss or hug.

My Light felt jagged, tearing at my skin from the inside, when I denied the contact by stepping out of his reach.

His face fell. "You didn't like the quartet?"

"Did I enjoy being woken up at seven on my one morning off? Did I enjoy having four random dudes at my door ready to sing some bullshit song that you thought would make me forget everything? Do I enjoy having my two Bonded Variants at each other's throats? Do I enjoy having so much fucking Light coursing through me that it feels like I'm going to burst? No, Mason! I am not having a good time right now!" I didn't realize how much my voice had risen as I ranted, but a chorus of laughs and *oh shits* coming from the crew alerted me to our audience.

Mason glanced behind himself and rubbed the back of his neck, looking appropriately chastised and embarrassed.

"Go back to work, Mason," I grumbled, rolling my eyes. I refused to apologize, and I was even more irritated that I was about to walk away unsatisfied—again.

"I'm on my break. I have some time if you want to talk, or whatever."

Walk away, Oriana. He's not going to tell you what you want to know. There was no point trying to get anything out of him in the middle of his workday, but another idea formed in my mind.

"Is there somewhere more private we can go?" I glanced at the workers.

With a smile, Mason took my hand and led me across the street. There was a shipping container across from the construction site, its doors open and building materials visible on the inside. The back of it faced the woods. It was risky, but it would do.

I was still mad, but that didn't stop the Light from

57

straining to get to him, making it hard to focus on anything else.

Leaning back against the metal, I grabbed a loop in Mason's toolbelt and pulled him into me. The look of surprise was wiped right off his face when I wrapped my arms around his neck and pulled his mouth down to mine. One of his hands smacked against the wall next to my head for balance and the other grabbed my ass.

The Light practically sang at all that unfettered access to all that glorious bare skin. I ran my hands over his chest and back, let it flow.

It felt like a cool shower after a long day working in the sun. My whole body sighed in relief, even as it sang at his touch and begged for more.

Gripping his wrist, I guided his hand up under my skirt. He palmed my pussy and broke our kiss with a groan.

"Fuck, Oriana." He licked his lips and looked from side to side. It was broad daylight, and there was a construction crew mere feet away. I could still hear the power tools and voices in the near distance.

"Make me come before someone comes looking for you." I injected an extra bit of huskiness into my voice and rolled my hips, rubbing myself against his hand.

Mason didn't need to be told twice. He pushed my underwear to the side and spread the rapidly growing wetness to my clit.

He gyrated his hips against mine, his erection thick between us, as he rubbed me firmly. There was no time for buildup, not that I needed it. The Light, our connection, made everything more intense by default, and my climax started to build in no time.

I plastered my mouth to his neck to muffle the sounds of pleasure in my throat. Mason pushed two fingers inside and started pumping them while his thumb worked my clit. As the orgasm crested, tingles spreading through my whole body, I bit his shoulder and groaned, doing my best to stay as quiet as possible.

He let me ride it out before gently removing his hand from between my legs. My head thumped back against the container as I caught my breath. Mason continued to kiss up and down my neck, his hips still grinding.

Once I knew I could stand without collapsing, I pushed against his shoulders. He backed off, his eyes hooded.

I patted him on the shoulder, right next to the hickey I'd left there. "OK, thanks."

He frowned at me as I adjusted my skirt and retied my hair. "What?"

"I'm gonna head off. You better get back to work." Without a glance back, I walked away.

I was no longer frustrated—sexually or Light-driven—and I was still pissed at him. Let *him* deal with being left confused and unsatisfied for a change.

NINE

Over the next few days, I settled into a bit of a routine. I focused on my classes and studying, ignored Mason's and Leon's continued attempts at getting back into my good graces, and when the Light got insistent, paid one of them a brief visit. There was no talking, and I was the only one who left satisfied.

Was I using them? Yes. Did I feel bad about it? Maybe a little. But did I give them a chance to open up about their issues every time, only to be met with more silence? You bet your ass, I did.

I knew this wasn't sustainable. We couldn't live the rest of our lives with this stunted, frayed kind of relationship, but I was so close to graduating after busting my ass for years, and I'd be damned if I let a couple of stubborn assholes derail that. Even if they were permanently Bonded to me by the power of the Light itself.

It was after dinner as I knocked on Leon's door. I had classes the next day and he had work, so I nearly didn't come over, but the Light was starting to do that buzzing thing under my skin, and I couldn't afford a sleepless night.

The lock clicked, and his face appeared in the crack.

"Oriana," he said in a flat, unimpressed voice.

"Leon." I nodded, matching his tone.

He stared me down, but after a beat, he sighed and opened the door fully, standing aside to let me in. As I knew he would.

"Wanna talk, baby?" I asked as he closed the door.

"Just come here," he grumbled, but his deep breath, with his nose buried in my neck, was full of contentment.

I pulled his mouth to mine, and he gave me what I wanted, his tongue swiping against mine as he lifted me onto the kitchen counter. Kneeling before me, he pulled my shorts and underwear off in one go.

They were both frustrated by my stonewalling, but just as I couldn't ignore my Light-fueled need to be near them, they couldn't resist giving me what I needed.

Leon caressed my thighs from the knees to my bare aching core . . . and paused. He pressed his forehead to my leg, and something in the air shifted.

I ran my fingers through his hair, not demanding anything—just caressing his scalp gently, reminding him I was here.

He looked up at me, his gaze full of uncertainty and other emotions I couldn't pinpoint.

"I . . ." He licked his lips.

I gazed back patiently.

"He . . ." He gritted his teeth and tried again. "Mason and I, we . . ."

"Maybe I'll put my pants back on and we can sit on the couch?" I suggested, walking the line between creating an open space for him to talk and lightening the mood just a little.

Leon gave me a small smile and got to his feet, then helped me down and passed me my shorts.

"We were actually friends once, Mason and I," he began, leaning his head on the back of the couch. I sat still, hardly breathing. "But I guess that's part of the problem, because the people closest to you, the ones who know you best, are the ones who know how to hurt you the most."

Ominous beginning. I was hooked already.

"We met when we were fourteen or fifteen, maybe. There was this skate park in the West Village. It was near my school and Mason's mom's work, so we were there at the same time a lot, and we eventually started hanging out. It was a whole group of us, but Mason and I kind of clicked for some reason, even though we were from totally different worlds."

"Maybe because you're both mine, even though none of us knew it then," I suggested.

"Yeah, probably. Funny thing is, I actually really wanted to go to Bradford Hills Institute, but I would've had to board, and my mom thought I was too young. She was a little overprotective. I think maybe it was the Light drawing me to you, but when that wasn't possible, it drew me to Mason."

I nodded. It made a lot of sense. I'd been attending BHI since I was twelve.

"Anyway. We were a group of unsupervised teenagers, so it's no surprise we did some stupid shit. Not least of which was starting fights. My ability made for great entertainment when some unsuspecting dude took a swing, then was shocked to feel like he was the one getting pummeled. I learned to take a punch at an early age."

I frowned and took his hand. Despite his ability, that statement didn't sit right. But he kept speaking, and I didn't want to interrupt him when he was finally telling me what I wanted to know.

"I'm not saying I'm blameless in what happened, Oriana." He looked at me with a devastating expression in his eyes, and I rubbed his hand, my heart breaking before I even knew the full story. "I made some colossally dumb decisions. I was a prick, but what fifteen-year-old isn't? I didn't take shit seriously when I should've, Mason's brother got involved, and I can totally understand why he'd be protective of his little bro—that's his family. But what Mason did?" Leon shook his head, a muscle in his jaw twitching. "He took it too far. He's the reason you and I were kept apart for so long. It's his fault I didn't find you sooner."

"What? How?" I was beyond confused but hanging on every word.

"There was this girl, Jenna." My expression must've shown the irrational pang of jealous rage I felt at the mere mention of another woman, because Leon took both my hands in his. "This is part of the reason why I didn't want to tell you any of this—this look on your face. Because no girl, no relationship or fling or anything, could compare to you. Nothing comes even close to how I feel about you now, Oriana. You're my whole world."

His words soothed my burning envy like a balm, so I nodded for him to continue.

"But at the time, I really thought I was falling for her. I had it bad. The kind of crush that only feels that intense when you're a teenager. And I'd finally gotten up the guts to ask her out. We'd been on a few dates, and I'd fallen even harder. And then Mason . . . he was more pissed about his little bro getting into trouble with us older kids than I realized. He went after Jenna, really put the charm on, and managed to get her to dump me and be with him. Then he went to my dad and embellished some of the stupid shit I'd done. My dad is a proud, hard man."

And the reason Leon had to learn how to take a punch early on, I suspected.

"Dad was furious, worried about me tarnishing his reputation. Even Mom's pleading couldn't change his mind. She'd been reluctant to send me to Bradford, only a few hours' drive away, but I ended up being sent to France instead. In the space of a week, I lost my girl and got sent away from my friends and family."

I couldn't imagine how hard that must've been for him. A young boy with an abusive father, heartbroken and alone in a foreign country. I climbed into his lap and ran my fingers through his hair, letting my Light flow freely. The tightness around Leon's eyes released, and he relaxed against me.

"Mason didn't know I was his Vital though, right? Or yours. He wouldn't have been able to stay away from me. Not to mention, if we'd met, I would've known too." I kept my voice gentle, trying to worm in a thread of the other side of the story, even though I still didn't know it all yet.

"No, of course not. None of us knew until we met recently. But when I saw him in the city that day and I realized he truly was your Variant"—Leon shook his head—"all that shit with Jenna came back, all the betrayal and anger. He took her from me, and I care more about you than I ever could've about her. I know it's irrational, but I was terrified he would take you from me too. He nearly did. You were ready to break up with me after you met him. He didn't even know we were seeing each other, and he nearly took you from me. It felt like my whole life was crashing down around me all over again. I felt like I was sixteen again and about to lose everything I cared about."

I drew him in for a tight hug and held on for a long time. When I pulled back, I made sure he was looking me in the eyes, really listening, before I spoke.

"You're not going to lose me, Leon. I'm your Vital. You're my Variant. We're irrevocably Bonded by the Light. You know that, right? I'm not going anywhere."

"I know," he said, his voice strained, as he wrapped me up in another tight hug.

I had so many questions. I wanted to know more about what his father had done, what Mason had told him, how Mason's little brother was involved, where this Jenna was living these days. But Leon looked absolutely drained when he finally released me from his grip.

"Will you stay the night?" He gave me the puppy-dog eyes. "I miss you. Please."

It was an easy decision to stay. He'd been vulnerable with me and told me what I wanted to know. There was nowhere I'd rather be than in his arms all night.

TEN

The next day I paced the stretch of concrete in front of my res hall. It was a balmy evening, and the setting sun cast the campus in warm golden light.

I'd asked Mason to meet me at my place after he got off work, but I was driving Ebony and Crystal to distraction with my nervous energy, so I went downstairs to wait for him. I knew I needed to talk to Leon more, but I also wanted to hear what Mason had to say.

"Oriana?" Mason's curious voice had me spinning to face him. I'd been so up in my head I hadn't even noticed him approaching.

"Did you come straight from work?" He had his steel-capped boots on and his backpack slung over his shoulder, and he was all dusty.

"You wanted to see me, so . . ." He shrugged. "Work ran late, and I didn't want to give you time to change your mind." His half smile was uncertain and hopeful at the same time.

"Leon told me about Jenna." I just put it out there, releasing a big breath as I did. I hadn't realized how much the tension of knowing just one side of the story had been getting to me.

Mason adjusted his grip on his backpack, pursing his lips slightly. "What did he tell you exactly?"

"That he was falling for her." I had to swallow before continuing. It was hard talking about one of my Variants having feelings for another woman. "And that you deliberately took her from him." I left out the part about how that experience had made Leon worry about losing me now. It felt too intimate a thing to share when they were still so hostile toward each other.

"That's all he told you?" Mason scoffed.

"He told me a little about how you met too, that you used to get up to stupid teenage boy shit."

"Stupid teenage boy shit." He shook his head, running his tongue over the underside of his bottom lip.

"Mason, I know I don't have the full story. I wasn't there. I'm not trying to . . . I didn't call you here to have a go at you or anything. I just—"

"You just want me to defend myself, is that it? You want my side of the story because you want to know that your Bonded Variant wouldn't do something like that, right? You want to know that I'd never be so manipulative as to deliberately take another guy's girl, hurt her to hurt him. Well, I'm sorry to disappoint you, Oriana, because I did that. I *am* that guy. And I'm not sorry."

"OK . . ." My heart was racing, my mind struggling to reconcile this callous attitude with the Mason I knew. Or at least thought I did. Was our Light-driven connection warping my view? But how could this be the same guy who'd pushed himself past his limits to save a pregnant lady the night we met?

A couple walked past, heading into my res hall, and they looked in our direction curiously.

I waited for the door to close behind them before moving away from the entrance and toward a nearby bench. "Do you want to sit? Tell me what happened."

"No, I don't want to sit," Mason snapped, and it hurt to hear him using that tone, even if it wasn't exactly directed at me. He dropped his backpack to the ground and ran his hands through his hair. "Did Leon tell you what this *stupid teenage boy shit* was?" He spat the other man's name as though it tasted sour on his tongue.

"Something about starting fights. He didn't go into detail."

"Of course not." Mason rolled his eyes. "Leon and his douchebag, rich kid buddies went around starting fights. No one was ever ready for his ability. So, while Leon goaded innocent people into hitting him and getting hurt just as bad, his friends would record the whole thing and put it up online. Most of the time, they'd pick people who they thought were human, and usually, they were right. So Leon would heal faster with his Variant DNA, and these unsuspecting schmucks would end up with weeks of bruising or broken bones or permanent scarring."

I cringed. I couldn't imagine Leon hurting someone so badly—even if it was his ability doling out the damage originally directed at him.

"One day, they provoked a kid from my school. But, of course, the video started with the kid throwing the first punch and left out everything that had gone down before. He got expelled. I tried talking to Leon, explaining to him that what was a bit of fun for him was honestly wrecking people's lives. I thought he'd actually listen since we were supposed to be friends, but he didn't give a shit. So I told his mom. He was pissed, and next thing I know, the job my mom had just been offered at Bradford Hills Institute was withdrawn. She could never have afforded to send me here, but working for them would've meant a serious discount in fees and a big pay increase. You and I could've met *years* ago."

I squeezed my eyes shut for a moment, just letting the anger and frustration course through me. They'd both unwittingly kept each other away from me.

"That was the end of our friendship. I was done with him and his bullshit, but my little brother . . ." Mason sighed. "He's not a Variant, but he is hotheaded. He took a swing at Leon, and we both know how that works out for humans."

I winced.

"Leon was fine, but my brother fell awkwardly, hit his head on a brick. He's fine now, but the hospital bills nearly ruined my mother. So yeah, I took his girlfriend. I was a dumb teenage kid too, and I wanted to hurt him like he'd hurt my family. And yeah, I went to his dad because I didn't know what else to do. How the fuck was I supposed to know the asshole would send Leon to France?"

"Jesus fucking Christ." I rubbed my face, releasing a massive breath as I tried to process all this. "It escalated pretty severely then."

"Yeah, shit escalated. But what *he* did seriously affected people's lives. What *I* did doesn't even compare. I stole a girl he was never going to end up with anyway." He gestured at me. "He was sent to a fancy school in another country. Big deal. He still got the girl of his dreams and held on to all the privileges his birth afforded him."

"You're both adults now," I hedged, unable to resist trying to bridge this gap between the two most important

69

people in my life. "I think he feels really bad about what he did back then."

"Are you seriously defending him right now?" Mason took half a step back, his eyes widening.

"No!" For the first time in weeks, I was the one reaching for him, and he was the one avoiding my touch. "I'm not excusing what he did, but—"

"But nothing! He—you know what? I don't want to argue with you." He snatched his backpack up from the ground.

"Mason, where are you going? Please don't leave. Let's talk about this more." I hated the desperate edge in my voice.

"Not right now, Oreo." His gaze softened, but he still wouldn't touch me. "It's become glaringly obvious the two of us need to hash this out first. I'll call you tomorrow."

He pressed a rushed kiss to my forehead and walked away with purpose in his gait.

I was getting what I'd wanted—for them to talk about their issues. But as I stood there watching Mason's tense back as he left, I didn't feel relieved or even hopeful for progress.

Dread sat heavy in my gut. I feared I'd pushed them into a confrontation that would just make everything worse.

My eyes stung as I made my way back upstairs, but I managed to hold the tears back until I was in my room.

ELEVEN

I was halfway through a pint of ice cream when my phone went off and I lunged for it. All my calls and texts to both Mason and Leon had gone unanswered, and I was wallowing like a pro. My roomies had offered to stay in with me like the good friends they were, but I knew they both had plans, so I shooed them out before burying my woes in icy sweet goodness.

My shoulders sagged when I saw a text from Crystal. Scooping another massive mouthful of ice cream into my gob, I opened the message.

Crystal: Hey girl. We ended up at The Hole. Thought you'd want to see this.

The Hole was as charming an establishment as its name suggested. It was dirty, rough, and attracted a dangerous crowd.

I couldn't believe what I was looking at. The photo had been taken from a distance, but it clearly showed Mason talking to one of the staff, a gym bag slung over his shoulder, and there was no mistaking Leon's glare from behind the same dude.

What the hell were they thinking? Did they actually call each other up to plan a damn fistfight? Or did one of them follow the other there?

It didn't really matter how they both came to be at a sketchy underground Variant fight club. Clearly they were planning to beat the living shit out of each other, and no one had bothered to tell me.

I growled and punched my pillow before kicking the blanket off violently. Muttering curses under my breath, I pulled on a pair of ripped jeans and a tank top. My black Valentino ankle boots completed my hastily assembled outfit, and I grabbed a BHI hoodie off the back of my desk chair as I stormed out.

Fuming the entire way, I broke speed limits as I drove to The Hole. Half of me was furious and having fantasies of knocking their heads together in that cage myself. The other half—the Light-fueled, Bonded half—was beside itself with worry. They were *mine*, and I couldn't stand the thought of them getting hurt—even if they were the ones doing the hurting.

The fact I cared so much only made me angrier, which made it harder to control the flow of Light I drew into myself, which only made me crave them more, and around and around we went.

Gravel went flying under my tires when I pulled into the dingy parking lot. I hastily parked and marched up to the unassuming door in the squat building.

A tall man with a gut stepped out of the shadows: the bouncer. "You got ID, girly?"

"You got a liquor license, big guy?" I shot back with a smirk. Nothing about this place was legal. "I never get asked for ID when Billy D's on the door," I added. The only way into this place your first time was to show up with someone who'd already been. After that, you needed to know a bouncer's name, be convincing enough that you weren't a cop, or have a wad of cash at the ready.

At my mention of Billy D, the bouncer visibly relaxed and waved me in.

As I jogged down the stairs, the music got louder, mixing with the heady noise of the ravenous crowd. They were drunk on cheap liquor and violence. The cage on the lowest level of the club—the centerpiece of this dump of an establishment—was empty, except for a young man mopping up what looked like blood. I assumed I'd arrived at the end of a fight.

After shoving through the crowd, I gripped the metal railing and scanned the two levels, but it was too packed to pick out any familiar faces. I pulled my phone out and shot off a quick text to Crystal.

Me: I'm here. Did they fight?

Crystal: No, not yet. Where are you?

I ignored the question and started making my way down the levels. My best bet to intercept them, if they were planning what I thought they were planning, would be to get near the entrance to the cage and wait there.

But I was still too far away when the lights trained on the cage turned brighter, announcing the beginning of the next fight.

Mason climbed into the cage, Leon following closely behind. They were both shirtless and shoeless, wearing nothing more than shorts and mutual disdain. Bookies started moving through the crowd to take bets.

"Stop!" I shouted, panic rising. "Wait! Mason! Leon! *Stop!*"

The clamoring crowd and the music drowned out my

yelling. I shoved people out of the way, trying to rush to the cage, but no one seemed to give a shit.

The crowd erupted in a cheer, and my panic practically choked the air out of my lungs. I'd made it to the ground level, but the crowd down here was even more dense, and I couldn't see over their heads. The only thing I could hear was the occasional rattle of the chain-link fence that composed the walls of the barbaric fighting cage.

People shouted encouragements and taunts between waves of cheering. I just focused on squeezing through one gap after another to get closer to my idiot Variants.

A deafening roar went up from the audience, and I looked up, fear skittering down my spine.

The light above the fighting cage had turned on. It was connected to sensors that detected the distinct energetic signature of the Light. The aim of the fights was to win *without* using one's ability—a show of both control and physical dominance. One, or both, of them had used their ability.

Before I could panic more—wondering if Mason had broken Leon's back with his super strength, or if Leon's ability had them both equally hurt—the spectators stopped cheering, and a general hum of confusion spread throughout the room.

With the energy of the onlookers less intense, I could finally push my way right to the side of the cage.

They were both sweaty and breathing hard. They looked as if they were fighting to the death.

Mason was baring his teeth in a snarl, his mouth bloodied. Leon's left eye was puffy and half swollen closed. They both had flecks of blood on their chests, arms, fists.

I gripped the fence, the chain-link digging into my fingers.

"Stop," I tried to shout, but the word came out on a desperate croak. They were the ones throwing punches to guts, but it was my breath that had been taken away.

I looked around frantically, but no one was paying even the slightest attention to me. I wasn't the only one pressed up against the cage, gripping it, shaking it, shouting things. The three refs—If you could even call them that—were gathered at the door to the cage, talking in a rushed manner while their eyes darted between the crowd, the fight, and the light above the cage.

I glanced up again. It was still shining bright but . . . I mentally slapped a palm to my forehead. They were both Bonded to me. They both had my Light coursing through them. Their abilities couldn't hurt each other.

At the realization that they came here knowing that, a spike of anger, burning hot, sliced through all the anguish in my chest.

Leon landed on his back in front of me, making me gasp. Mason was on him instantly, throwing punches at his face and upper body.

This close I could hear the smacking of knuckles on flesh, could hear their grunts and growls, could smell their sweat.

"Mason! Fucking stop!" I shrieked so loudly that even a few people on the opposite side of the cage looked away from the fight to stare at me.

Mason whipped his head up, fist raised, and his eyes met mine. He blinked, as if he wasn't quite sure I was actually there.

Leon had his arms up, protecting his head, and hadn't noticed me yet. Taking advantage of Mason's momentary distraction, he jerked up and managed to throw Mason off. Mason smacked into the fence right in front of me, and

Leon used his momentum to follow through with a brutal punch. Mason's head snapped to the side, and blood splattered onto my cheek.

I screamed.

All the emotions that had been building up since I realized they were here—hell, since they'd met and started tearing my heart down the middle—burst out of me. The pain, anger, frustration, worry, love, anguish all came tumbling out on that scream.

Leon jerked back, his shocked eyes connecting with my wild gaze.

It wasn't until I let everything loose that I realized how desperately the Light had been straining to flow out of me, to get to my Variants. They were hurting, and the Light wanted to heal them, soothe their pain.

The bulb above the cage, the one rigged to detect Light, exploded. Sparks rained down as I breathed hard, tears mixing with blood on my cheeks. It wasn't my blood, but it felt as if I was the one bleeding out anyway. My fight was draining out of me.

The door to the fighting cage opened, and the refs rushed in, not that Mason and Leon needed separating. They were both crouched on the floor of the ring, watching me with matching horrified, pained expressions.

As the refs ushered them out, they both looked over their shoulders to keep me in sight while I scrambled through the crowd to follow. It wasn't hard. People shuffled out of the way so I could pass. The refs must've realized what was happening, because one of them showed me down a dingy corridor.

I followed my Variants into a room, and we were left alone, the door closing with a click. The sound of the crowd, the thumping music, became instantly muffled.

I wanted to scream again.

"Oriana?" Mason approached slowly, bending to the side to catch my eye.

"What are you doing here, baby?" Leon asked, his tone just as gentle.

I looked between them, their faces and bodies hurting, wrecked at each other's hands. Anger warred with desperation inside me, and it came out in the form of sobs.

They moved for me at the same time.

"Don't touch me!" I screeched, and they recoiled. "I'm already wearing your blood." Smacking a hand against my cheek, I swiped at it and held my reddened palm out for them to see.

"Every time you hurt each other," I wailed through my unstoppable crying, "every time you say mean shit, or avoid each other, or *hit* each other—you're hurting *me*. Can't you see that? You're. Hurting. Me." I thumped my messy hand against my chest with each word.

At least they had the decency to look appropriately chastised, even sorry. They exchanged a worried look, bare chests still heaving from the fight.

Mason blinked and swiped at his right eye as blood trickled into it from a gash in his head. I zeroed in on that wound, one of many, and whimpered. It was a pathetic sound, but it reflected how brittle I felt inside.

Cursing under his breath, Leon went to rummage through something on a nearby bench. He came back to press gauze against Mason's bleeding head. His other hand held an icepack against his own swollen left eye.

Something inside me settled, soothed by the sight of them not only coexisting in the same room but actually *fixing* each other. I moved forward and placed a palm on each of their shoulders, letting the Light flow for a few moments.

They weren't depleted, but their Variant bodies would heal much faster than any human could, and that took energy too. I couldn't help craving to aid in the process. The calm inside my chest increased, and they both sighed softly at the contact. Light transfer between Bonds was comforting just as much as it was useful.

They needed me, but I needed them too. Both of them, in harmony—not the way we'd been stumbling along so far.

Leon winced as he flexed his free hand. It was bruised and the knuckles were cut up. I glanced at Mason's hands, relieved to find his weren't as bad. I looked to the ample supply of first aid stuff on the bench, wondering what I needed to fix Leon's knuckles. I didn't have any experience patching people up after they'd been beaten to a pulp. But I also couldn't seem to make myself break contact with either of them.

Mason must've seen the frustration in my gaze. With a small sigh, he reached over and grabbed more gauze and a bottle of something. Keeping one hand on Leon's shoulder, I moved the other up to hold the gauze at Mason's head. With his own resigned sigh, Leon lifted his hand for Mason to disinfect and tape up.

Slowly, if reluctantly, they tended to each other's wounds bit by bit. Antiseptic cream was administered, cuts and scrapes cleaned, Band-Aids and dressing applied. Just as surely as they'd inflicted pain on one another, they soothed the wounds they'd put there.

And in the process, they soothed a deeply hurting part of my soul. I just stood there, letting my Light do its thing while I watched my two Variants silently care for each other. Even if they were only doing it because I was on the verge of breaking down.

They took turns holding me while the other dressed and collected his things. Still not speaking, we left through a back entrance and made our way through the parking lot. I held both their hands, still struggling to let go.

When we got to Leon's car, I panicked a little.

"No." I gripped Mason's hand so tightly he winced. "Don't go. I can't . . . I need . . ."

Mason caressed my cheek, watching me with worry deep in his eyes.

I forced myself to complete a sentence. "I need you both. I can't be away from you right now."

Mason looked up, having some kind of silent conversation with Leon over the top of my head.

Leon caressed the back of my hand with his thumb. "We can stay at my place."

After a beat, Mason nodded. "I'll drive. Your hand is too busted."

To my utter disbelief, Leon didn't argue. He threw the keys to Mason and got into the back seat.

TWELVE

I woke up alone in the middle of Leon's bed. Sighing as I stretched, I hadn't felt so rested in a really long time. Sleeping between your two Bonded Variants really did wonders for a girl's REM cycle.

We'd fit comfortably in the king-size bed, and the Light felt settled in a way it hadn't since before I'd met either of them. Not that I needed the reminder, but clearly, having them both close was good for the Bond— good for all of us. If only those two stubborn dickheads would accept it.

As I got out of bed, the sound of soft male voices drew my attention. I tiptoed to the ajar bedroom door and peeked out.

Mason and Leon were sitting on opposite ends of the couch, slumped back against the cushions and avoiding looking in each other's direction.

"Hockey?" Mason said.

Leon scoffed. "If I wanted to watch a bunch of dudes whale on each other, I'd just go to The Hole again." He took a sip of whatever was in his mug. "Tennis?"

"Eh. Don't really know the rules." Mason shrugged. "Rugby?"

Leon sighed, and I could hear the edge of frustration in his tone. "Nah. What about lacrosse?"

"*Lacrosse?*" Mason lifted his head to give Leon an incredulous look. "Tell me you have a trust fund without telling me you have a trust fund."

"Forget sports then." Leon put his mug on the coffee table.

"Well, we couldn't find a single food we both like, or a movie, or a song, so . . ."

"There's gotta be something we can agree on."

I'd heard enough. I quickly used the bathroom and got dressed, the contentment I'd woken up in draining away bit by bit, pushed out by my growing resentment.

They couldn't find a single thing to agree on? I could appreciate them trying to find some common ground with something small—something that didn't matter. It was actually a good place to start. But they'd clearly been at it for some time, and neither one had been able to let go of his stubbornness long enough to admit they both liked pizza. Everyone fucking liked pizza!

I stormed out of the bedroom and put my shoes on as they both got to their feet.

"How about boxing? Huh?" I blurted before they could say anything. "Wrestling? Karate? UFC, maybe? I know for a fact you both enjoy dudes whaling on each other. Or maybe you only like fighting when you're the ones throwing punches."

"Oreo—"

"No!" I cut Mason off. "I can't believe that after last night you can't find even *one* tiny little thing to agree on. It's like you don't even give a shit that this is hurting me."

"Baby—"

"Fuck you!" I cut Leon off too. I was nothing if not fair. "You don't get to call me baby—or Oreo," I snapped in Mason's direction before stomping to the front door. "Don't follow me."

I slammed the door shut.

Leon's apartment building was in a quiet part of Bradford Hills and a good twenty-minute walk from campus. I considered calling a car but decided against it. It was overcast but not raining, and the brisk walk might help me work some of this anger out.

I could've gone through town, to the main entrance to BHI, but I decided to take the back way and go through a side gate. I really wasn't in the mood for bumping into anyone. It would be hard enough telling my roomies about the shit show that was last night. I had a stupid number of messages in our group chat and a few missed calls.

The back way took me through the industrial part of town—blissfully deserted on a Saturday morning—and once my hands weren't shaking anymore, I replied to my friends to let them know I was on my way back. Only the occasional car or van drove past on the quiet road. Mechanics, wholesalers, and other businesses sat dark and empty on either side of me, their roller doors firmly closed. There was one café on the corner, but even that was closed on weekends.

My pace slowed to something more measured about halfway up the long road. The walk was doing what I'd hoped it would, and I was cooling down. Now that the fog of hurt and anger had cleared a bit, I even started to wonder if I'd been too harsh with them. I'd only heard a snippet of their conversation, and they were kind of trying to get along in their own stupid boy way.

A car drove past, drawing my attention. There was

nothing remarkable about it—a blue sedan with what looked like two people inside, driving at a normal speed. I couldn't put my finger on it, but something about it made me watch it a bit closer. I could've sworn the passenger turned in my direction as they passed.

Just as I told myself I was simply on edge from the current Bond situation, the blue car turned into what looked like a driveway to one of the businesses. It was more than two blocks away and I couldn't make out the details, but I could see enough to know no one got out.

Something wasn't right.

I considered turning down the next street, but I had no idea if it was a dead end or where I'd end up. Keeping an eye on the car, I slowed my pace and grabbed my phone.

The car reversed and started driving back toward me at a much slower speed. An unpleasant, icy feeling slithered down my spine.

I dialed Leon and held my phone to my ear. It rang once, twice . . .

The car stopped about a block away, on my side of the road.

On the third ring, Leon picked up.

"Something's wrong," I rushed out before he could even say hello.

"What? Where are you?" He sounded immediately alarmed.

"Dells Road. There's a blue car. It drove past me, then turned around and drove back toward me, and now it's stopped about half a block away."

"I'm coming. Stay on the phone, Oriana." I heard shuffling, a door closing, Leon speaking to someone. "Can you see who's in the car?"

"Two people. I can't tell . . ." I'd slowed to barely a

crawl, my instincts telling me not to go near the car. It was still running, the two shapes in the front just sitting there.

"Can you make out the license plate?"

"Uh . . ." I squinted and came to a complete stop. "Something, UB75, maybe? There's definitely a nine at the end. It's too far away, and I don't want to go any closer."

"It's OK, don't go closer. Turn around slowly."

Heart hammering in my chest, I did as he said.

"Start walking back the way you came. Keep it casual."

"OK. OK." I could hear my heavy breaths making that grating sound through the speaker. "I don't like having them behind me."

I glanced back over my shoulder just in time to see the car lurch forward.

"Fuck!" I started running. "They're coming toward me."

"Oriana! Run!" That was Mason's voice on the other end now. I did what he said and what my body demanded I do anyway. I *hauled ass*, pumping my legs, my boots slapping on the concrete. "We're nearly there!"

The blue car drove right past me, and for a quick, suspended moment in time I thought I must look so ridiculous. *It's driving past. They're probably just lost. They must think I'm some kind of lunatic sprinting up the street.*

But then it skidded to a stop, one wheel up on the sidewalk, and the doors opened.

"Oh my god!" I nearly fell trying to stop so abruptly, but I managed to stay on my feet as I turned and started running in the other direction, not sparing a second to get a look at them.

My phone was clutched in my hand, no longer pressed to my ear, all my focus on getting the fuck away! But I could still make out Mason's voice yelling down the line.

"Run, Oriana! Kick, punch, scratch—whatever you have to do to buy some time! *Scream!*"

I screamed.

The shrill sound echoed off the deserted, utilitarian buildings, mocking me. *Scream all you want—there's no one around to hear you.*

A body slammed into mine, knocking me off balance but catching me before I fell. A hand wrapped around my mouth. I couldn't see the guy behind me, but the one in front of me had a bandanna pulled up over his nose, and he slapped my phone out of my hand.

I bit the hand over my mouth as hard as I could, tasting blood. The guy behind me cursed and removed it, and I screamed again. I screamed until my throat was raw.

The second dude grabbed my legs and lifted me up between them. I screamed some more, thrashing my arms and legs, bowing my back, making myself as difficult to handle as I possibly could.

I'd managed to run a half-decent distance from the car, but they were still managing to drag me toward it.

THIRTEEN

I let my body go limp, becoming dead weight. They scrambled to hold on, and the one with my legs lost his grip.

I kicked back at the guy behind me as the one in front scrambled to catch me again. All my focus had narrowed in on my two attackers, my surroundings fading into the distance. So I was completely stunned to suddenly see Mason. He tackled the guy trying to grab my legs, and then I heard Leon's voice shouting something.

I was dropped like a sack of potatoes on the hard concrete, wincing at the pain that shot through my tailbone. Scrambling backward, I scraped my palms on the rough pavement as I took in the scene with wide eyes.

The guy that had grabbed me from behind swung at Leon, who could've probably dodged the punch but stood there and took it. It landed square on his jaw and snapped his head to the side. Leon's opponent yelled out in pain and reeled back, gripping his jaw in the same spot.

The other attacker recovered and ran at Mason. Mason dropped his shoulder and picked the guy clean off the ground, lifted him over his head, and threw him as if he were a ragdoll and not a full-grown man. He landed on the hood of the blue car.

My attention snapped back to Leon, who was now landing punch after brutal punch on the guy who'd attacked him.

Mason rushed to my side, his expression as panicked as I felt. I clung to him as he helped me to my feet. In the next moment, Leon was there too, saying soothing things I couldn't quite process.

They surrounded me with their warmth and care and protection.

I could hear car doors closing and tires screeching as sirens approached, but I didn't look up. I buried my face in someone's shoulder and let them hold me.

"This is ridiculous. I'm fine," I insisted for the hundredth time.

Mason and Leon had taken to ignoring me. As we entered the emergency room, Mason hovered so closely I felt like a baby taking her first steps. Meanwhile, Leon rushed up to the triage desk.

I rolled my eyes and sat in an ugly plastic chair in the waiting room. I had a headache, likely from the adrenaline crash; my muscles were sore; and the scrapes on my hands stung. But nothing was broken or bleeding. This was overkill. Figured that the first thing they agreed on was in direct opposition to what I wanted.

And I wanted a nice hot shower and my own bed.

The police had shown up moments after my attackers drove off. They sent a car after them but couldn't find them.

I was asked a bunch of questions while Leon and Mason refused to leave my side. Then a couple of black-clad Melior Group dudes showed up and asked the same questions and then a few more.

They'd all barely gotten in their cars to leave—after taking photos and repeating the questions for the third time —when my Variants started insisting on a trip to the hospital.

"Oriana Roy," a nurse holding a clipboard called.

My guys sprang to their feet, took an elbow each, and started helping me up.

The nurse came over. "Do you need a wheelchair?"

"No." I wrenched my arms free and softened my tone. "No, thank you. I don't really think I need to be here, but my . . . Variants insisted."

"I understand." He gave me a gentle smile. "Let's get you checked out anyway, OK?"

A doctor's checkup, several scans, and many hours later, I received the all clear. To be fair, a cut on my leg did need a few stitches, but other than that I was fine.

"See? I'm fine." I huffed as the nurse left my curtained bed area to grab my discharge paperwork.

Mason and Leon looked ragged—clothes wrinkled, hair a mess, and what seemed like bone-deep exhaustion in their expressions. I felt bad for arguing about the hospital visit so much. That would've been a harrowing experience for them too.

I couldn't imagine getting a call like that from one of them, hearing them scream on the other end of the line. They must've been so scared.

I shuddered.

"Are you OK?" Mason took my hand. Leon perched himself on the other side of my bed.

"I'm fine." I said it firmly but much more gently, looking them both in the eye one by one.

"Oriana!"

I whipped my head up at the sound of my name to find the curtain around my bed shoved aside. My brother appeared behind it.

"Hey, Xavier." I gave him a lame little wave.

"Jesus fucking Christ." Xavier shuffled Mason out of the way and hugged me tightly. Then he crossed his arms over his chest, giving me a hard look. "What the hell happened? And why didn't you call me? Why did I have to find out my little sister was in some kind of attack from dickheads at work? And who are these two assholes?"

"This is Mason and Leon." I pointed at them in turn as I started to get off the bed. All three men moved to help me, and I smacked at them until they backed off. "As I'm sure you can guess by their overprotectiveness, they're my Bonded Variants."

"Your . . . *what*?" Xavier gaped at me. "When did this happen?"

"It's recent." I searched the ground for my shoes, and Mason dropped them at my feet.

"Like, in the last few days? Because we talked last weekend, Oriana. You might want to call Mom, by the way. Mom and Dad are both losing their shit."

"Oh fuck! You told them?" I glared at my brother. "I was going to wait until I was out of the hospital before calling them."

Xavier just shrugged. "Might wanna call them sooner rather than later. I'm pretty sure Dad was shouting at some poor airline employee over the phone, demanding they create a seat on a fully booked flight."

I groaned and twisted around, looking for my purse.

Leon handed it to me, and I dug my phone out. I had thirty-seven missed calls.

Xavier shook Mason's and Leon's hands as I called my parents. They were beside themselves, but I managed to convince them I was neither dead nor dying. They still wanted to come see for themselves, but I explained that I had a lot going on, and we arranged for them to come visit in a few weeks—with the strict proviso that I promptly answered calls and texts and let my brother know immediately if something was wrong.

While I was on the phone, the nurse came in with paperwork and told me I was free to go, so the four of us made our way toward the parking lot. Xavier chatted with Mason and Leon the whole way, as if they were bros.

So, they could participate in the same conversation for my brother but couldn't hold back from punching each other in *my* presence? Nice.

The cool evening air blew the messy bits of my hair off my face as we emerged from the building. I stopped and faced the three of them with my hands on my hips.

"Stop being nice to them," I barked at Xavier.

"OK . . ." He looked uncertain.

"I knew I'd found my Bond weeks ago. I didn't tell you or Mom and Dad because it's been a fucking nightmare."

Leon winced, while Mason hung his head and stuffed his hands into his pockets.

"Turns out they've known each other since childhood and they hate each other," I went on. "And apparently that's more important than me."

I told my brother about everything—how we met, what they'd told me about their pasts, even the bullshit from The Hole last night. God, had it only been twenty-four hours? I kept it brief but covered the main points.

Maybe it was shitty of me to tell my brother their private information—*our* private issues—but I was bruised and beaten in more ways than one, and I felt as though no one was on my side. I just needed someone on my side.

When my eyes started to sting with unshed tears, Xavier wrapped an arm around my shoulders and glared at my Variants. I leaned against his familiar frame. Xavier may have teased me and given me hell while we were growing up, but he'd always been there for me when it mattered. He was a douchebag in the way all big brothers sometimes were, but he protected me and loved me unconditionally in the way only family could.

"You two realize this is for life, right?" Xavier looked at my guys pointedly. "I know you all just met and you're young and not thinking about the long term, and that's fine, but you're *Bonded*. There's no breaking that. You're going to be connected for life. I'm not saying you can't live apart—it's been done—but it's not pretty. And the stronger your Bond, the worse it will be if that's where this goes."

The tears fell; the thought of not being with them hurt worse than anything those two masked men could've done to me. I knew it was an option, but I hadn't considered it. I *wanted* to be with them.

"Now, I don't know the full story of your beef," Xavier continued, "but is it worth losing a lifetime of being happy with your Bonded Vital? Do you know how few people *have* a Vital? And you two dickheads are pushing yours away because of some shit that went down a decade ago? Be together, don't be together—whatever. But pull your heads out of your asses and figure it out soon. Because if you keep hurting my sister . . ." Xavier paused and took a deep breath. "Well, let's just say, I personally know Alec Zacarias."

Mason and Leon visibly blanched. Leon had started his

new job just a couple months ago, and Mason had moved to Bradford Hills only a few weeks back, but they both already knew of the Master of Pain. Alec Zacarias worked for Melior Group, like my brother, and his ability was to inflict pain. Merely touching him had made people faint, and he could cause pain just by looking at someone. You did *not* want to be on his bad side.

"Come on, Oriana, let's get you home." Xavier made to turn away.

"Can you just give us a minute?" I gave him as confident a look as I could muster, wiping the tears off my face. He nodded and shot the guys one last glare before walking to a bench far enough away that we could talk privately.

I took each of their hands and let the Light flow freely. This would be the last time I'd be transferring Light to them for a while—possibly forever.

The events of the past twenty-four hours had brought things into sharp focus for me. And Xavier's evaluation of the whole situation had solidified what I'd been thinking about in the hospital for hours. There was no point in delaying it.

"Oriana, I don't want to lose you." Mason squeezed my hand, as if I'd evaporate if he released me.

"*We* don't want to lose you," Leon added, holding on just as tightly to my other hand. "We're trying. We were trying to find some common ground this morning."

Mason nodded. "Yeah, we want to make this work. It's just not easy."

"It's not easy for me either." I forced deep breaths into my lungs, holding the overwhelming emotion back so I could say what I needed to say. "But we can't keep going like this. It's not fair to any of us."

"Please . . . *please* don't leave me." Leon's eyes started to water as he looked at me with desperation.

"I just found you, Oreo." Mason sounded just as panicked.

"I . . ." I licked my lips. "I'm falling for you both. I want to be with you. Completely, in every Light-given and other way possible. But Xavier was right. If we keep spending time together, sleeping together, transferring Light and strengthening the Bond . . . it's only going to hurt more if you two can't figure this out and find a way to live with each other in harmony. I don't even want to *think* about going against the Bond. I can't even imagine how horrible a life without you would be, but I have to consider the option. And so do you."

They both started protesting, talking over each other.

"Stop!" I cut them off, drawing a worried glance from my brother. "I need some time. I need you two to take some time. One month, no contact. And let me make this perfectly clear—*I'm in*. I am all in with both of you. But I do mean *both* of you. I want it all, or nothing at all. This shit we're doing—the push and pull, the half-in and half-out relationship, the avoiding the real problem—it's toxic. So I want you to take the month and figure out what you want. If you can't find a way to move past your issues, then that's the end for us, and if you can, I need you to come back to me a month from now with a solid plan. I need to know you can find a way to work it out."

I dropped their hands. They were both crying now, as if I was dying and not asking for one month of space.

"One month." I turned and rushed away. It was the hardest thing I'd ever done, walking away from them, but it was what we all needed. One way or another, in a month, I'd know what the rest of my life would look like.

FOURTEEN

I sipped on my third glass of champagne, wondering if I could leave yet. The fundraising gala's formal dinner and speeches were over, and everyone was dancing and milling about the lavishly decorated ballroom.

It had been three weeks since I'd given Mason and Leon my ultimatum—three agonizing weeks without my Bonded Variants.

I was doing my best to brace for the worst. Of course, I hoped beyond hope they'd miraculously find some way to work out their hatred for each other, but I was preparing to say goodbye to them in another week.

Which was why I sat in my midnight-blue silk ballgown at a mostly empty table, playing with the candle wax that had dripped down the gold candelabra and talking to Crystal and Josh Mason.

"Ugh. Yeah, I just hope Professor Jenkins can learn to end a lecture on time. I'm constantly late to my next class after hers," Josh said. We had some of the same classes and were friendly. He was a nice guy—smart and good-looking, even with his neat blond hair and preppy put-together look.

But he wasn't my Variant. The handshakes and casual touches we'd exchanged were enough to make that clear. It felt nothing like touching Mason or Leon.

"I'm just glad she uses examples more recent than the eighties. I don't think Professor Granger gave a single case study of a business owned by a woman before he retired," I replied. Josh was easy to talk to, but I couldn't stop thinking about how his last name was Mason . . . I missed *my* Mason. I missed them both so much it hurt.

"Yeah, well, he's gone now, and his poor wife is the only one who's forced to listen to his nasally voice," Crystal said, and we all chuckled. Josh glanced over her shoulder for what felt like the hundredth time since we sat down. He'd been watching Eve Blackburn dance with Dot during our whole conversation. Eve had started at Bradford Hills Institute a few months back—probably around the time I met Leon. Ugh! Everything reminded me of them, dammit.

Quick! Think about something else. I followed Josh's gaze to the pretty brunette swaying her hips. Ethan Paul was watching her too, but then, she was his girlfriend. I wondered if he was aware that his best friend had the hots for his girl.

Crystal, along with a good portion of the BHI female population, was not happy about this development. She glanced over her shoulder, and I caught her little eye-roll as she turned back and started talking about something else.

I smirked behind my champagne flute before taking another sip. The bubbles tickled my throat. At least they served the good stuff at these overpriced events. It may have been a gala to raise funds for some senator who pushed Variant rights in her political career or something—I wasn't really interested in politics—but these events always served the secondary purpose of allowing Variants to mingle in the hopes of finding their Vital.

I had my two troublesome Variants already, but it couldn't hurt to mingle. Maybe I'd find a third one who would miraculously find a way for the other two to live peacefully. Wishful thinking—most Vitals had one or two Bonded Variants, rarely more. Anything over three was almost unheard of.

But thinking about it was a good distraction. Just like getting dressed up and hanging out with my besties had been. And just like my parents' upcoming visit would be. They were arriving tomorrow and would leave just before the ultimatum deadline I'd given the guys.

I sighed and stabbed the bit of wax with my nail. Not for the first time, I questioned my decision to give them an ultimatum in the first place. Maybe it was too harsh. Maybe I was pushing them away unnecessarily. Maybe they just needed more time to adjust to being in a Bond. Or maybe that was the Light talking—railing against the very idea of being away from them, let alone permanently. I'd had to get the girls to physically block the door on several occasions so I wouldn't rush out and go to them.

Thank fuck for my roomies. I had no idea how I would've survived that period without them. They listened to me rage about the unfairness of it all, stopped me from calling them. Ebony gave me her perspective from another Bonded Vital, and Crystal was happy to take the excess Light that inevitably built up when I let my guard down.

"Hey, girls!" Ebony's sudden appearance made me sit up straight. "And Josh."

"Hey! You guys having a good night?" I tried my best to make my smile appear natural. I was miserable most of the time, but I tried not to burden my friends with it too much.

"Yeah, a little *too* good." Ebony cringed, but the amusement was clear in her sparkling gaze as she glanced behind her. Kylie was swaying on her feet, supported by Derek. He looked bored out of his mind but had only smiles for the two women in his Bond. "Kylie drank her weight in Dom Pérignon. We're heading back to the hotel."

"Can I grab a lift with you?" Crystal stood with a sigh. "This evening's a bust."

"Sorry the conversation wasn't stimulating enough for you." Josh chuckled, getting to his feet.

"Nothing personal. I'm just disappointed your bestie is off the market." Crystal pouted, and we all turned to look at Kid watching Eve as if there was no one else in the room.

"Yeah. You and everyone else . . . ," Josh muttered, something complicated in his gaze. "I'll see you guys around."

He sauntered off as we waved him away, and I pushed my chair back.

"I'll come too. If you're all leaving, I have zero interest in hanging around," I said, smoothing the fabric of my gown. When no one replied, I looked up with a slight frown.

"You sure about that?" Ebony's gaze flicked to mine, then back to something behind me.

I looked over my shoulder, and my breath stuttered in my chest.

Mason and Leon were walking into the ballroom, shoulder to shoulder. It was unfair how good they looked in their tuxes, with their hair neat and their shoes polished. Leon was in a classic tux, with the bow tie and the white shirt, while Mason had opted for an all-black look, including the tie and pocket square.

They stopped just inside the doors, spoke to each other briefly, then scanned the room. Mason pulled at his collar, frowning, and even from this far away, I could see the exasperated sigh Leon released. He adjusted his cuff links and muttered something that had Mason glaring at him.

Nothing had changed. So why were they here, together?

Mason spotted me and nudged Leon. As one, they marched in my direction, weaving through the opulently dressed crowd.

A small, warm hand took mine, and I glanced over to see Crystal at my side.

"Want us to stay?" Ebony asked from my other side. "Or get you out of here?"

I shook my head and battled to get my breathing under control. Now that they were here—mere feet away and closing in—I didn't have it in me to walk away. The Light simply wouldn't allow it.

"Oriana," Leon breathed as they came to a stop before me. This close, I could see they looked as nervous and uncertain as I felt.

I shook my head. "No, it's only been three weeks. This isn't . . . I'm not . . ."

"We know," Mason rushed out. "But we did what you asked, and we couldn't wait any longer."

"It was too hard," Leon agreed. "We've made a decision, and . . . we would've been here sooner too, but there was a wreck on the freeway and—"

Mason elbowed him in the side. "Doesn't matter now."

"Right. Never mind that."

I raised my eyebrows at Leon's agreement. "What the fuck is happening?" I murmured, more to myself than anything.

Leon glanced to either side of me, and I realized my friends were still there.

I dropped Crystal's hand and turned to face them. "You guys head off. I'll be fine."

"You sure?" Ebony asked, frowning.

I nodded. Reluctantly, they moved past.

"God help you both if she's a wreck at the end of this," Crystal muttered as she passed, but the two men at my back didn't reply. My heart wedged itself in my throat, because that was a very real possibility.

But I couldn't just stand there and ignore them.

Conflicted as I was, I turned.

They both stared at me, and my panic started to rise as the silence stretched on. They were struggling to start the conversation because it was going to be a hard one to have. It was over.

Finally, Leon nudged Mason, and he cleared his throat.

"Right. Uh . . . Oriana. Oreo." His voice and his gaze softened at my pet name. "Will you dance with us?"

Leon held his hand out like a perfect gentleman. I blinked down at it. What? I thought they were here to make up—or break up. Not *dance*.

"Please, baby," Leon pleaded with his eyes and his words.

The potential to be hurt and humiliated in public was making me jittery, but I had to believe, at the very least, they wouldn't do that to me. They wouldn't get all dressed up and break up with me in a crowd of the most prominent members of Variant society in the tri-state area. *Right?*

I placed my hand in Leon's.

He led me out to the middle of the dance floor, Mason staying close at my back. My heart beat so hard in my chest I worried it might crack a rib. I kept glancing at the glittering crowd around us, but no one was paying any attention.

There were other Bonds dancing in threes, and no one was privy to the turmoil writhing inside me.

My attention snapped back to Leon as he expertly maneuvered me into a twirl, my gown swishing out around me. Instead of landing against his chest, I ended up facing Mason instead. He smiled at me, the emotions in his eyes too many to name.

Leon stepped in close at my back, and I shivered at his heat, his proximity. He dragged the backs of his fingers down my arm, leaving goosebumps in his wake. With a gentle grip on my wrist, he lifted my hand and placed it in Mason's waiting one. His other hand found mine at our sides, our fingers twining together. Each man's free hand landed on my waist, and I was surrounded by them, by leather and vanilla and tangerine and cedar, my Variants, my Bond.

I couldn't hold the Light back any longer, not when it was trying so hard to burst through my skin it almost hurt.

Mason closed his eyes briefly, his face going slack, and Leon released a breath that tickled the back of my neck. I couldn't help the little moan that escaped my parted lips. Thankfully, the music was too loud for anyone to hear me.

How the fuck was I supposed to let this go and live my life without them? It felt as if my head had been held under water for three weeks, my only oxygen coming through a thin straw, and now I'd burst above the surface to take greedy lungfuls of air.

They *were* like air. I needed them to survive.

It was too hard . . .

Leon's words from earlier haunted me. What was too hard? Their issues? Being with me? I couldn't stand this any longer.

They moved as though they'd practiced it, and we all

started swaying, slowly turning. I squeezed their hands—not willing to let go, preparing to let go.

"Please . . ." I met Mason's gaze, the word trailing off. I had no idea what I was even pleading for. *Please just put me out of my misery. Please don't leave me.*

Please don't break my heart.

Mason licked his lips and nervously glanced over my shoulder before speaking. "Oriana. These past three weeks have been torture."

I scoffed. "Yeah, I know."

"Being without you felt like suddenly missing a limb."

"Like I couldn't breathe properly," Leon added, and I gasped at how accurately he reflected what I'd just been thinking.

"It was made even worse because I was forced to spend every free second of it with Leon."

My jaw clenched. I really didn't want to hear more bullshit about how much they hated each other—especially while they had me boxed in. But Mason forged on.

"I've been staying at his place. We agreed that we needed to spend every spare moment we had doing what you asked. So, any time we weren't working, we were together, talking, arguing, just . . . *trying.*"

"And?" I forced myself to ask.

"And it went about as well as you can imagine." Mason grimaced. "We were at each other's throats and getting nowhere. There's a lot of resentment between us, a lot of hurt in our history, years of pent-up anger and pain."

I froze, bringing our rhythmic movements to a halt. "I can't do this. Don't do this to me here." I half pleaded and half demanded. What the hell were they thinking?

They both stepped impossibly closer, sandwiching me

between them, making it impossible for me to get away, to think, to breathe.

No—I breathed *easier*. And I hated and loved it in equal measure.

"But," Mason said firmly, forcing my gaze back up to his. "After about two weeks, we realized we couldn't do this alone."

"I can't solve your problems," I gritted out. "I shouldn't have to."

"We know, Oreo," Mason said, gently, reverently brushing a bit of hair off my forehead.

I gasped as they moved in sync again, taking me completely by surprise as they worked together to move me into another dramatic spin. This time, I ended up facing Leon, Mason at my back. They coaxed me into a slow dance.

"We know this isn't your problem to solve," Leon said. "But we acknowledge that it affects you more than anyone else. And we are *so sorry* that this bullshit between us has ruined these first few months of being Bonded for you."

"*So* fucking sorry." Mason pressed his forehead to the back of my head for a moment.

"But the fact remains that we can't figure this out on our own. So, after constantly being at each other's throats for two weeks straight, we agreed on something for the first time ever. We needed help. So we got some."

"What does that mean?" I asked.

"We reached out to a therapist who specializes in relationships and Bonds counseling."

"You did?" Hope soared, making me feel as if I were floating on air between them. But it also felt as if it might burst at any moment, and I'd drop in a broken heap as they walked away.

"We did." Leon gave me a small smile. "She was able to fit us in for an emergency session right away."

"And then another three," Mason added. "We've been going to intensive therapy all week."

"So that's it?" I frowned. "One week of therapy and you think this is all fixed now?"

They both laughed, their big, solid bodies shaking.

"No, baby." Leon cupped my neck. "That's just the beginning. We know we have a long way to go, but we're willing to put in the work."

"For you." Mason squeezed my waist.

"And for us."

"If you haven't changed your mind, that is."

"If you're in, we're in."

"We want to make this work."

It took a few moments for it all to sink in. I'd been putting so much energy into not getting my hopes up, into preparing for the worst, that my mind struggled to register the exact opposite was happening.

They weren't walking away from me; they wanted to be with me, were willing to work through their issues to make it happen, had even managed to come to me as a united front after only three weeks instead of four.

Visceral relief washed through my body. I trembled as I released a massive breath and my knees went weak. But I wasn't at the slightest risk of falling, because they had me. They had my back and my front, and they worked together to hold me up.

As they would for the rest of our lives.

I lifted onto my toes and wrapped an arm around Leon's neck. With one hand still holding Mason's, I pulled Leon down for a kiss.

He kissed me sweetly, his lips soft against mine, but his

fingers dug into my neck and my waist as if I might dissolve in his grasp.

"Oh, baby," he breathed once we pulled apart, wiping away a tear I hadn't even noticed slipping out.

Instead of pulling me in for another kiss, he shocked the hell out of me by nudging me to turn around. Mason wrapped an arm around my waist, and I welcomed his kiss too. He was more forceful, less appropriate than Leon, but I melted into his embrace.

I couldn't care less what anyone thought, if anyone was looking at us, judging us, or maybe even envying us. Because I had what I'd always wanted, and nothing else mattered.

"Get me out of here," I demanded, panting against Mason's lips.

He grinned. "Yes, ma'am."

With my hands in theirs, the three of us rushed out of the ballroom and into the New York City night.

FIFTEEN

The reality of the situation started to settle in as Mason whistled for a cab and Leon draped his jacket around my shoulders.

They weren't leaving. I wasn't losing them. I didn't have to figure out how to live my life without two pieces of my soul. The relief and pure joy of it made me giddy, and I found myself giggling as we piled into the back of a taxi.

Of course, we had a long way to go, boundaries to navigate, therapy to sit through, a life together to figure out. But we were all willing to put in the work. Because what we had was special. It was ordained by the Light itself.

We had something worth fighting for.

I was worth fighting for. Their earnest words and loving touches as we drove through the city were proof.

The cab dropped us off at a very nice hotel. The lobby was surely elegant and lovely, but I hardly noticed it as we rushed to the elevators. I was too wrapped up in my Bonded Variants, in my own happiness.

We had the elevator to ourselves, and I was struck by the reflection in the smoky mirror. Me in my blue gown,

Leon on one side, Mason on the other. We looked good together, right, *natural*. I threaded my fingers with Mason's and leaned my head on Leon's shoulder, smiling at myself in the mirror.

"Beautiful." Leon smiled at me in the reflection, then planted a kiss on my head.

"Perfect." Mason lifted our hands and kissed the back of mine.

I sighed, the sound content rather than frustrated for the first time in weeks.

The room was spacious and comfortable, with a view of the city sparkling beyond. Once again, I didn't take in much of the details, too focused on my Variants. There was only one lamp on, casting the space in a soft, warm glow.

Draping Leon's jacket over the back of a chair, I stood at the window and took it all in.

"Are you hungry?" Mason asked, shucking his own jacket and loosening the tie. I shook my head.

"What do you want to do?" Leon asked.

It was late, but I wasn't tired. I was too amped to sleep. So were they, judging by their wide-open eyes and energy.

I turned to face them. "Actually, there is something I'd like to do, but . . . uh . . ." I scratched at my scalp under the elaborate updo. The bobby pins were digging in.

I hadn't thought before I spoke, and now uncertainty glued the words to the inside of my throat. I wasn't sure if they were ready for it.

My Light was both satisfied and needy, ecstatic to have my Variants so close but also wanting more. It was pushing me to give them all of me. And I'd be lying if I said I didn't want the same thing. Light-driven instinct aside, I wanted them. Together.

I'd been with them separately; I knew how they could

make me feel. The mere thought of having them at the same time, with nothing between us—physically or figuratively—made my inner muscles clench involuntarily.

But I didn't want to push them. If I ruined the progress they'd made because I was horny, I would be so mad at myself.

Leon slid his hands into his pockets and turned a knowing smirk in Mason's direction. "Told you."

Mason rubbed the back of his neck as he met Leon's gaze, his lips quirking up tentatively. "Shit. OK. Yeah, let's do this."

"Wait." I shook my head, clearing the lust and confusion. "Just so we're on the same page, you guys talked about . . ." I raised my eyebrows, deliberately letting them fill in the rest.

"Sharing you?" Leon's voice dropped into something deeper, suggestive. Of course they'd talked about sharing me —my time, my affection, my Light, my life. He knew very well I was asking about sharing me *physically* now.

"Yes, we discussed it," Mason confirmed, matching Leon's intensity. "At length. I didn't think you'd want to *bond* like that with us both so soon, but Leon was confident you would."

"And you're both OK with it? You're into it? Having sex with me at the same time?" I needed to be sure.

They both nodded, the heat in their eyes solidifying the confirmation.

I released a shaky breath and shifted on the spot. My skin warmed just from having them both look at me so . . . *hungrily*.

"You discussed it at length, huh?" My own voice became husky, my breathing shallow with anticipation. "What exactly did you talk about?"

Leon cocked his head to the side. "You like that, baby? That we talked about you? Discussed how we'd both fuck you? Got hard imagining it?"

"Jesus," I breathed. "Yes, I like that a lot."

Leon stepped forward and wrapped an arm around my waist, leaving his other hand in his pocket. The move was confident, bordering on cocky, and it was really doing it for me.

"Are you getting wet for us?" He skimmed his nose up the side of my neck. I whimpered and rolled my head to the side, giving him more access. My gaze connected with Mason's, and whatever he saw in my face had him moving toward me. He crowded me in from behind, his hands gripping my hips.

It was intoxicating being surrounded by them like this. My heart, my soul, my Light, *everything* was drunk on them.

But my brain hadn't completely succumbed, and a tiny sliver of fear sobered me up enough to ask: "Are you sure? Are you both comfortable with this? I don't want sex to ruin things. I . . . I can wait for the physical stuff."

Leon pulled back to give me a more serious look. "Oriana, we discussed it. We know what we're comfortable with."

"The focus is on you." Mason squeezed my hips to emphasize his point. "That's something we agree on without question." He started carefully pulling the pins from my hair, making me sigh as it released around my shoulders bit by bit.

"Nothing is going to get between us anymore," Leon said. "I promise."

"So do I." Mason massaged my scalp now that its metal prison had been removed.

"We know each other's boundaries. The rest is up to you. If you want this to stop at any time, just say so. We just want to make you feel good."

A loaded pause stretched between us. They were waiting for my lead, making sure I was ready. Their assurances that they were on the same page, that I wouldn't lose them again, were all I needed to completely lean into this moment.

"Do you want this to stop?" Leon's eyes narrowed, and a smirk creeped up his cheek. He could see it in my face, the surrender, I was sure of it.

"Don't stop." I managed to say it firmly, confidently, even though I was quaking inside.

"Then answer the question," Mason whispered in my ear, making me shiver. What question? "Are you wet for us, Oriana?"

All I could manage was a breathy moan and a nod.

"I think that was a yes," Leon said against my lips before licking them. I leaned forward, desperate for a kiss, but he backed up.

"If she can't say it, maybe we should find out for ourselves." Mason licked the side of my neck before gently sucking on that curve between my neck and shoulder.

I rubbed my thighs together, eager for them to find out just how much moisture was pooling between them. If they kept licking me like that, it was going to start dripping down my thighs.

Mason gathered my skirt up around my waist as Leon took half a step back. He raked his gaze over my body before reaching between my legs. He cupped me there, his fingers barely moving. One hand still remained in his pocket, and there was something insanely hot about that—the way he just stood there so confidently, his posture casual, while he held my pussy in the palm of his hand as though he owned it.

Probably because he did. They both owned me now, body and soul.

"She's completely fucking soaked through her underwear," Leon groaned, his voice giving away that he wasn't as cool and collected as he appeared.

Mason smiled against my throat; his teeth gave the sensitive skin a light graze.

Leon nudged my underwear to the side and slid one finger up and down, playing with the wetness.

"Fuck, so slick. You have to feel her." He looked at Mason over my shoulder, and the fact they were communicating in a positive way, with me between them, turned me on just as much as all the dirty talk.

Mason held as much of my dress as he could in one fist and joined Leon's fingers with his own. They both explored me, their fingers gliding between my folds with ease, teasing at my opening, brushing over my clit.

I leaned my head back against Mason's shoulder, my hips rolling on instinct, my body begging them for more.

Leon dropped to his knees and gently helped me step out of my heels. He watched me reverently from below as he pulled my underwear down my legs. With a firm grip, he lifted my left leg and settled it over his shoulder. He didn't break eye contact until he leaned in and buried his face in my sex, disappearing among the blue silk.

I cried out as his mouth connected with me, his lips, tongue, and even teeth getting right to work. No more teasing; they were delivering on all that pleasure they'd promised, and my body was ready. I was so keyed up, so turned on, that I was close to orgasm within a few strokes of his skilled tongue.

Mason turned my head to the side and kissed me, *devoured* me. His hand dragged down my throat, my chest, and grabbed my breast. He squeezed and caressed it as both their tongues drove me wild—one on my lips, one on . . . well, my other lips.

I threaded my fingers into Leon's hair, ruining his neat style and tugging sharply, keeping him in place. I moaned my release into Mason's mouth. Pleasure shot through my body, and the Light zinged in every spot where they touched me.

Leon sat back on his heels, breathing hard. His eyes burned with desire as he wiped my arousal off his chin.

Mason lowered the zipper down the back of my dress as Leon stood up. I was completely nude for them now, and they were still clothed. It felt deliciously lewd—the fabric against my sensitive skin, their erections extra rough against me as they crowded me once more, grinding their hips.

But I wanted them as naked and bared for me as I was for them. I tugged at their shirts, reaching behind me awkwardly for Mason's.

"Clothes off," I demanded, my voice breathy.

Instead of doing as I asked, they moved to stand side by side in front of me, then shuffled me backward to the bed. My knees hit the edge of the mattress, and they pushed me back, their hands supporting and caressing as they guided me to the middle.

They backed off to stand at the foot of the bed, and both men watched me intently as they removed their shirts.

"One more for me," Mason said, licking his lips, as he stroked his bulging erection over the fabric of his trousers. Leon copied the motion, and they both stood there, staring at my naked, needy body as they touched themselves.

"Come in Mason's mouth, then you get to see these

cocks." Leon gave himself a firm squeeze, just in case I wasn't sure which cocks he was referring to.

They climbed onto the bed. Mason settled between my legs, while Leon crawled to my side.

Leon hitched one of my legs up and out, holding me open for Mason. Mason shifted partially onto his side, his elbow at my hip and his hand pulled up just above my clit. His body pinned me down, while his other hand teased at my entrance.

"Fuck, so wet for us," he groaned as he pushed two fingers in.

"And she tastes fucking amazing." Leon leaned down and kissed me firmly, giving me a sample of my own flavor on his tongue.

Mason dived in. The firm strokes of his tongue matched the strokes of his fingers inside me. Once again, they had me on the edge of orgasm in a matter of moments.

Leon released my mouth so I could pant and moan, moving instead to my breasts. He licked and sucked one while caressing the other, then pinched the nipple until I arched into the hint of pain.

I tried to squeeze my legs together as I came, the pleasure almost too much as it washed through my body and coalesced between my legs. But they had me pinned open, and I had no choice but to scream and surrender to them.

As I panted, Mason sat up and licked his lips, then sucked his fingers into his mouth. The way they were acting, you'd think I tasted like caramel or something.

But I couldn't think about that now. Because they were on either side of the bed, dropping their pants and delivering on their promise. It was a king-size bed, and I had no chance at reaching them both.

My head whipped from side to side. They were both so

hard their lengths practically stood up vertically. Leon was a little longer, but Mason had that girth. They were perfect for me—together, reaching every part of me from the inside that craved to be filled.

My Light strained against my skin for them again, as if it hadn't been given free rein and unrestrained access for the past hour. My body was writhing, ready for more despite the two orgasms.

I whined—a pathetic, desperate sound in my throat—at having them out of reach. It was simply impossible to pick one over the other, reach to one side instead of the other.

Without any words spoken or looks exchanged, they climbed onto the bed on either side of me. They caressed and kissed and nuzzled—their actions more comforting than sexual for a few moments. They knew what I needed, and they were giving it to me.

In that moment I knew, somewhere deep inside, that I'd never have to choose again. I was theirs and they were mine. The Light felt as if it expanded in my chest, something fundamental settling in the Bond between us.

I didn't have time to examine it though, because their attentions were turning heated once more, their hands greedy for my body, their mouths devouring mine. No more dirty talk or teasing or pretense. We were moving on pure instinct now, in tune with one another.

I wrapped my fingers around their lengths, pumping slowly, reveling in how solid yet smooth they felt in my hands. There was something incredibly empowering about having two strong men grasped in your fists as they grunted and their eyes fluttered.

We fed off one another, hyperaware of the slightest movements. Leon helped me sit up and position myself over

Mason's lap as Mason held his hard cock upright for me. A perfect, irresistible invitation.

Leon cupped my sensitive flesh from behind, leaving a wide gap between his middle and index fingers. He could feel me stretch as I lowered myself onto Mason, could feel the other man's cock sliding in easily. If it bothered either of them that Leon was basically touching Mason's dick, they didn't let on. All I heard and saw from them was pleasure, appreciation, *lust*.

I slid all the way down, relishing the way Mason's girth stretched me. Leon removed his hand just in time as I took Mason as deep as he could go.

Mason's fingers raked through my hair, and he pulled me down for a tender, all-consuming kiss. After a moment, my hips started to roll gently in rhythm with our tongues. He released my mouth, panting as he pressed our foreheads together. Then he pushed me to sit upright.

Leon had settled behind us, and he pulled me back against his chest, my back arching. Mason gripped my hips. His fingers dug in as he encouraged me to move, grind, bounce. I let my head roll back against Leon's chest and gave in to the sensations, letting my body chase the pleasure however it wanted.

We were a writhing mess; our moans filled the room, and the sheets twisted beneath us. Their hands were everywhere—in my hair, around my neck, tweaking my nipples, gripping my waist, caressing and fondling and driving me higher and higher and . . .

"Fuck!" I yelled as yet another orgasm took me by surprise. It surged through me, violent in its sudden force, drawing keening, guttural sounds from my throat.

Leon pushed me forward and pinned me between them, while Mason pumped up into me in wild, jerky movements. And then he was coming too, his chest bowing up off the bed, his neck muscles taut.

I needed to catch my breath, but I didn't want to. Because I *needed* Leon even more. I started to lift myself on shaky arms, and Leon helped me. Mason's cock slid out as I got my knees under me, and I whimpered at the sudden emptiness.

Leon was right there though, steadying me. For a moment, I thought he would maneuver me onto my back—it was probably a good idea, considering how my limbs were shaking—but I needed him *now*.

I arched my back, unashamedly presenting my aching pussy to him. With sudden desperation in his touch, Leon gripped my shoulder and positioned himself behind me. Pulling me back, he thrust his hips forward and rammed right into me in one swift, needy movement.

Mason brushed my hair out of my sweaty face, looking up at me with serenity and awe in his eyes as Leon took me from behind. He set a fast, punishing pace, his hips snapping forward.

I leaned down and kissed Mason, but I couldn't keep it up long. The new angle had Leon hitting some spot deep inside me that no one had ever reached, and I needed my mouth to pant and moan.

Mason gathered my hair up and swept it to the back of my head, and Leon took it in his fist. He pulled gently, making me arch even more as he fucked me like there was no tomorrow.

He was getting close; his movements lost some of that control, and his grunts took on a more urgent note. Mason tucked one arm under his head and dragged the other down the front of my body. He paused at my tits, feeling their weight as they swung with our movements, before reaching all the way down.

He pressed the tips of his fingers against my swollen clit and rubbed.

Leon and I came together, both of us crying out as his hips slammed into me one last time. He ground against me as if trying to get his whole body in there and not just his cock. Tears tracked down my face, the ecstasy drawing sobs from deep inside my chest as my body trembled.

Leon collapsed to the side, just barely managing not to fall on top of me. I rolled sideways too, and Mason shuffled so he was facing me with Leon curled around my back. We panted as we lay there.

My mind was completely blank, wiped clean by the four (*four!*) orgasms and the incredible sensation of the Light totally content and sated inside me. It got what it wanted, and so did I.

These men and I were Bonded, irrevocably connected for the rest of our lives. Logically, I knew there would be hurdles, issues to work through, differences to negotiate, but I also knew, deep in my bones, that everything would be OK. Because I was their Vital and they were *mine*, and nothing could come between us anymore.

THE END

Thank you for reading *Frayed Bond*! I hope you enjoyed Oriana and her infuriating men. If you're not ready to leave Bradford Hills and you need more of this Variant world, you're going to love *The Evelyn Maynard Trilogy*!

. . .

A captivating story about finding your soulmates in a world fought with unseen dangers, *Variant Lost* is an Amazon Top 100 bestseller!

One ordinary woman. Four extraordinary men. A power that could ruin them all.

Driven by a promise to keep her identity secret, tenacious Evelyn Maynard is all alone in the world. But a scholarship to the exclusive Bradford Hills Institute offers her a safe haven and a fresh start. Or so she thought. Eve is one of the only humans at her new school, brimming with those born with Variant DNA - and coveted superhuman abilities.

Bound by shared tragedy, Ethan, Josh, Tyler and Alec - and their unique powers - are revered amongst Variants. But something has always been missing and she may have just arrived with a scholarship and a glint in her enchanting, curious eyes.

Together, they could be unimaginably powerful, but being bonded by the Light itself isn't always a blessing, and Eve's dangerous past could curse them all.

Because she's not the only one keeping secrets...

Can they learn to trust each other in time to save themselves from an insidious danger no one saw coming?

If you enjoy books by Ilona Andrews, Jennifer L Armentrout, and KF Breene you'll love the rich world and complex characters in Variant Lost!

One-click *Variant Lost* now - https://geni.us/variant-lost OR, keep reading for the first chapter!

VARIANT LOST

One

I looked down at my watch: two minutes past midnight. It was officially my seventeenth birthday.

In the uncomfortable plastic seat next to me, my mother, Joyce, saw me checking the time. She kept her voice low as she reached for my arm. "Happy birthday, Evie."

"Don't," I grumbled and pulled my arm out of her reach.

She sighed and sat up straighter. To the casual observer she looked completely calm, sitting in the departures lounge at gate twelve at Melbourne Airport, her hands folded gently in her lap. It was a well-practiced mask—she was on high alert. We were sitting in seats with a wall at our backs as she scanned the airport every few seconds. Her oversized handbag was still slung over her shoulder, just like mine, in case we needed to move fast.

I bit down on my tongue to stop myself from crying. I was trying to be as alert as she was, but I kept thinking about the reason *why* we were at the airport, waiting to board a flight to Los Angeles with tickets purchased only hours before and new counterfeit passports tucked into our bags. I had committed a cardinal sin in my mother's eyes: I had made friends and got myself a boyfriend.

Naturally, we had to change our names and leave the country.

Ever since I could remember, my mother and I had been running, never staying in one place for longer than a few months, never getting close to other people. I was used to this routine, but this time I was more than just frustrated with having to start at another new school and memorize another new name. This time, for the first time, I was actually leaving something behind.

A flash of movement caught my attention and my mother stiffened, but she relaxed when she realized it was just a Variant, rushing through the airport at superhuman speed. The man in a suit had a panicked look on his face as he used his ability to get to his gate on time.

He was one of the approximately 18 percent of the world's population lucky enough to have Variant DNA, but his ability was a common one. I was just a boring human, a fact my mother was eternally grateful for, as it made it easier for us to blend in.

A painfully polite female voice came through the speakers: "Ladies and gentlemen, Qantas flight QF83 to Los Angeles will begin boarding shortly."

I tuned her out. I had taken more flights in my seventeen years than most people did their entire lives. I knew the boarding procedures better than half the ground staff.

I knew many things your average teenager didn't.

Instead of explaining the reasons behind our nomadic lifestyle, my mother had taught me how to be invisible. I knew to place myself near an exit in every building. I knew how to spot a person or vehicle that was following me and how to lose them. I knew how to completely wipe the memory of any electronic device. I knew how to forge official documents.

I knew everything except what I actually wanted to know—*why?*

I *didn't* know why my mother chose the places we went to over the years, zigzagging from one continent to the next. Until now, whenever I'd suggested America, she'd shut me down with a firm "no," but all of a sudden we were on our way to LA, and from there to Nampa, Idaho—a very specific location that I suspected was chosen very randomly.

Whatever the reason Joyce had chosen Nampa, the first leg of our journey was about to begin. Boarding had started.

With another surreptitious look around the airport, my mother placed herself behind me as we joined the line, shielding me from some unspoken potential threat. I rolled my eyes at her and faced the front as her dark blue eyes narrowed in exasperation.

I had the same eyes—dark blue—and just like her, you could see the blue in them only in natural light. I had her thick chocolate-brown hair too, but hers was cut short, and mine reached the middle of my back, falling in soft waves.

I was also just as stubborn. In a display of this trait, I crossed my arms over my chest and stared at my feet, concentrating on the swirls of little double helixes that littered my DNA socks. The machine ahead beeped rhythmically as the attendants scanned boarding passes, and I shuffled forward, wondering how such a great day had managed to turn to absolute shit in a matter of hours.

We had lived in Fitzroy, one of the most hipster suburbs of Melbourne, Australia, for almost eight months. Our moves hadn't been quite as frequent for the past few years. I was a teenager—moody, hormonal, and antisocial—which made it easier for my mother to prevent me from getting too close to anyone.

It's so much easier to make a friend at six than it is at sixteen. *Want to be my friend? OK!*—done deal. By the time you're in your teens, people have established friendships and years of shared experiences, and you're more aware of what others think of you. No one wants to disturb the delicate balance of their already angst-ridden existence by befriending the new girl.

Also, I had given up. With our next move always around the corner, I'd learned to make superficial conversation, seem friendly with a few people, but never truly get to know anyone.

Imagine my surprise when I not only made friends in Fitzroy but also got a boyfriend.

Somehow, Harvey Blackburn and his sister managed to weave their way into my solitary life. It happened slowly, over many weeks—sitting together in class, then at lunch, then chatting online. Then, somehow, Harvey and I were "a thing." I'd been on a few secret dates before, but none had gotten as close as Harvey. Harvey was the first of many things for me.

But even with the very first friends I'd ever made, I never spoke about our strange lifestyle in any detail, and I changed the topic when asked directly. I never invited them over. I rarely met with them outside of school, and then only when I was sure my mother was at work. I had to be careful. I burned to tell my mom about my first boyfriend, but I kept my mouth shut.

I'd been good at keeping my two lives separate, until earlier today.

Harvey, knowing he wouldn't be seeing me on my actual birthday, had pulled me around the corner of the

English classroom and presented me with a small gift box, his warm chocolate eyes sparkling with excitement. Inside was a charm bracelet with a heart charm attached.

I had never been given a gift from anyone but my mother. I was elated, and I slipped.

I forgot to take the bracelet off and hide it before going home. As if she was looking for evidence of my treachery, my mother spotted it as soon as I walked into the house. She came out of the kitchen, her eyes homing in on the offending jewelry.

I replayed the scene in my mind—my mother wiping her hands on a tea towel, her greeting catching in her throat as the smile fell from her face, the cold look in her eyes, the fear in her voice as she quietly asked, "What have you done, Evelyn?"

"*Miss?*"

We'd reached the front of the line. The attendant was looking at me expectantly, her palm outstretched. My mom nudged me.

I shook her hand off my shoulder and darted forward, passport and boarding pass in hand. "Sorry," I muttered.

The lady gave me a tight smile, scanned the boarding pass, and checked my fake passport with the efficiency of an often-repeated task. She didn't even hesitate before handing them back, and my heart sank yet again. A big part of me had hoped she would notice it was a fake and we would be forced to stay. The forgery was very good though; she had no idea. No one ever did.

I didn't return her smile as I moved past. Pausing as she repeated the process with my mother, I looked longingly back in the direction of the exit. I imagined myself pushing past the remaining passengers waiting to board and making a run for it, catching a taxi straight to Harvey's house.

It was a stupid fantasy.

With a shuddering breath, I followed my mother as she took the lead up the narrow corridor toward the aircraft. There was no going back for us—we never returned to any place we had previously lived in.

When I was younger, I used to cry and ask why I didn't have friends and why I didn't have a dad. As I got older, my questions became more specific. I asked why we couldn't stay anywhere for longer than a few months, why we couldn't use our real names, what or who we were running from in the first place.

My mother did her best to explain things to me without actually giving me any answers. It always came back to her fervent declarations that everything she ever did was for me. Her vague explanations just weren't enough for me anymore.

We trudged up the narrow aisle of the plane to our seats. I settled into the window seat, buckled my seatbelt, and turned away as my mother lowered herself into the seat beside me.

She sighed deeply and leaned over me, but she didn't touch me. "I'm so sorry, Evie . . ."

At least, for once, she wasn't making excuses. I glued my attention to the people in safety vests bustling about on the ground below. She had said those same words, but with a decidedly less gentle tone, only hours before.

We had spent the evening fighting, crying, and packing. As she'd yanked open drawers and shoved clothes into a bag, my mother had admonished me again. "How could you be so careless, Evelyn?"

"Careless?" I was sitting in the middle of the bed, refusing to participate in the packing. "I made some friends and got a boyfriend. And I didn't tell them anything!" I almost screeched in frustration, angry tears rolling down my red cheeks.

"I'm sorry, but that's just not good enough," she spat, not sounding sorry at all. She held her hands out, a bundle of clothing in each one, before letting them flop to her sides. "It would only be a matter of time before you slipped. That's what getting close to people does—it makes you let your guard down, and you tell them things about yourself. Deep, important things."

"What things?" I yelled as she resumed stuffing our belongings haphazardly into bags. "How could I tell them anything when I don't *know* anything?"

"We do not have time to have this argument again. We're leaving in twenty minutes. Anything you don't pack will be left behind."

We stared each other down, both of us breathing hard, both of us stubborn in our silence.

Finally, her shoulders slumped. "Please, Evie," she said quietly. Her wide eyes were pleading, and her hands had begun to shake. She was no longer mad at me; now she was just scared.

I was still mad at *her*, but I caved in and reluctantly got ready to leave. Again.

I didn't even get to say goodbye to my friends, to hug them tightly and say I'd never forget them. I'd tried to send a quick message to Harvey before my mother had burst into the room and confiscated my phone, wiping it clean and destroying the sim card.

The pilot's voice coming through the intercom as we taxied snapped me back into the present. "Welcome aboard flight QF83. My name is Bob Wheeler, and I'll be your captain today. Sitting next to me is Andy Cox, your copilot. Andy is a Variant with an ability to control the weather, so

I'm pleased to let you know that we can guarantee a turbulence-free flight tonight."

He continued to deliver the usual speech introducing the flight crew, but my mind was momentarily distracted, even from my ire at my mom. I had never met a Variant with an ability to control the weather, and I itched to research the science behind how it was possible, the impact it might have on weather patterns, the physics behind it all.

Science still didn't fully understand the Light—the energy that fueled Variant abilities and made it possible for people to control the weather, run faster than a Maserati, or read minds. It was a fascinating area of study. All sense of social propriety went out the window whenever I realized I was speaking to a Variant, and I would start firing all kinds of inappropriate and intrusive questions, my curiosity getting the better of me. I burned to ask the copilot how his ability worked, but I was strapped into an economy seat and had no way of making that happen. My mind returned to my previous miserable thoughts, and I slumped back with a sigh.

"That's an interesting Variant ability," Joyce piped up beside me.

I grunted and went back to looking out the window. She was making an effort, but I wasn't ready to let go of my resentment.

The plane took off, and everyone settled into the routine of a long-haul flight. My mother attempted to make conversation with me a few more times before finally giving up with a frustrated huff. I was determined to maintain my simmering outrage at how she had ruined my life, and I sulked, staring out at the pitch-black sky, forty thousand feet above the ground.

We were halfway across the Pacific Ocean when the plane crashed.

There was no warning—no time for anyone to wonder what was happening, get scared, hold each other. One minute we were gliding through the air, the next there was a loud *bang*, the plane lurched sideways, and we were plummeting.

I reached for my mother at the same time she reached for me, and we grasped each other's hands as our eyes met, wide with fear. There was no opportunity to say anything. No time to tell her the two simple things that actually needed to be said—*I'm sorry. I love you.*

A terrible metallic sound scraped against my ears, and then her hand was violently ripped out of mine, her mouth forming an O as she disappeared into darkness. The back of the plane had completely separated from the rest of it, as if a giant had torn it apart like a loaf of bread.

I stared at the emptiness next to my seat. There was the floor of the plane, there was my foot in my DNA sock (the shoe was gone), and there was the jagged line where the metal and wires and fabric had come apart, right between her seat and mine.

Beyond that there was nothing. Darkness.

We were still falling. People were screaming over the deafening whistle of rushing air as various items flew by me and out of the gaping hole through which my mother had disappeared. I focused on the jagged, torn edge of the plane, a piece of the carpet flapping furiously in the wind. My mother, my only family, was gone—probably dead. My mind couldn't process it, so instead, it helpfully supplied relevant statistics.

Statistically speaking, flying is the safest mode of transport.

The odds of a plane crashing are one in 1.2 million.

The odds of actually dying in a plane crash are closer to one in eleven million.

By comparison, the odds of dying in a car accident are about one in five thousand.

Just my luck that I would be on that one in 1.2 million flights.

As we plunged through the dark, I considered another number—2,130. The last time I had checked the in-flight information screen, that's about how many miles we were from Hawaii. I had calculated the distance, as it was the nearest land with things like hospitals and emergency response teams. Assuming the pilot had sent a distress call, it would be hours before anyone could get to us—if I even survived the crash in the first place.

I don't remember hitting the water. I remember the flapping piece of carpet by my feet, and I remember that useless information running through my head, but I have no recollection of the impact. After that is just disjointed flashes of memory.

The water was freezing cold. It felt like spikes of ice, all piercing my skin at the same time in a million different spots. People were shouting. Not many—nowhere near as many as were on the plane. I wore a life jacket. When had I put that on? Something was burning furious and bright nearby. I wanted to go closer to the heat, but I couldn't move. I couldn't do anything but shiver.

The fire was still there, but it had calmed down signifi-cantly. Like the embers of a campfire. No one was shouting anymore. The water rippled gently in front of me, calm and black like tar—impenetrable. I couldn't see even an inch past its surface. I couldn't feel my arms or my legs.

A light. Was it the fire? No, that had gone out a long time ago. It tinged the darkness. Violet. Dawn was coming. But that wasn't right either. This light was sharp, focused, and moving. There was a sound too—a loud whooshing from above. The water in front of my face rippled from the wind created by the helicopter blades. Helicopter! I had to look up, shout, wave, do something so they didn't leave.

I was being lifted into the light, but I was still cold and wet and I still couldn't feel my legs. The light wasn't warm and welcoming. It was harsh and bright, and the loud whooshing overwhelmed me. Someone lifted me from behind. An arm wrapped around my middle, holding me steady. The water seemed really far away now.

It was loud inside the helicopter. I was being jostled where I lay, tied down with something over my chest and hips. I couldn't see. My eyes were closed, and I didn't know how to open them. Voices shouted over the helicopter engine, only snippets of conversation.

". . . only survivors? Are you positive?"

"Yes." A firm "yes." His voice was clear, close. Strong and masculine, but smooth like warm honey. "We searched the whole area. Only her and the copilot. I don't know how she even survived. She was in the water so long."

Then a sliding sound and a third voice, farther away. ". . . in touch with her people . . . never got on the flight . . . last minute change of schedule . . . good intel, but can't predict . . ."

A hand landed on my calf. The man with the honey

*voice. I knew it belonged to him, but I didn't know how. It
was good that I could feel my legs again.*

~

When I woke up in the hospital, I had been asleep for
nearly two days, but I didn't know it at the time. They told
me all of it later. Nurses and doctors piled into my room,
marveling at the lack of permanent injury and my fast
recovery. Variants were more resilient against injury and
faster to recover, but I, as someone who was only human,
was lucky to have survived, or so the doctors kept saying. I
didn't feel lucky.

No. When I first woke up, it was only for a few
moments. The sounds came first: the soft thrum of
machines, a quiet beeping, muffled voices. Then I felt the
soft blankets and pillows under me.

I managed to lift my heavy eyelids and found myself
looking up at those corkboard squares that make up the ceil-
ings of hospitals and office buildings. The fluorescent light
was off, but it was still very bright in the room. It must have
been morning.

I angled my head down and scanned the space. There
was a door on my left and a window on my right, a hospital
tray on wheels under it. In the corner, next to the window,
was a chair. A man was sitting in it.

I could tell it was a man by the broad set of his shoulders, the muscles in his tattooed forearms. His elbows rested
on his knees, and his head was in his hands. He had dark
hair and a buzz cut. His fingers were digging into his scalp; I
had a feeling that if he had more hair, he would be pulling at
it. He was dressed in black: black boots planted firmly on
the floor, black pants, and a black T-shirt.

I tried to speak, but all I managed was a straggled inhale. It was enough to get his attention anyway. His head snapped up. He looked young, maybe in his twenties, but the look in his intense eyes gave me the impression that he had lived a thousand lifetimes while he'd sat in that ugly hospital chair. He had a five o'clock shadow covering his strong jaw and shocking ice-blue eyes. They pierced me, as the frigid water had pierced me.

"You're awake." I don't think he meant to say it out loud. It just came out on a breath. And then he was on his feet and next to my bed, leaning over me.

He reached a hand out as if to touch me and then pulled it back sharply. "I'll get a doctor." It was the man with the honey voice.

I was asleep again before he'd even left the room. The ice in his eyes was making me remember, and I couldn't handle it yet.

~

The next time I woke up, it didn't take me as long to gain consciousness.

I opened my eyes and lifted myself into a more comfortable position. I felt so much stronger than the first time, as if I didn't need to be in the hospital at all. It was dusk, the window on the right still letting in the fading light.

My eyes immediately went to the chair in the corner, but the room was empty, and for a second I wondered if I had hallucinated the man with the ice-blue eyes. Then I heard the tap turn on in the bathroom, and a moment later he walked out of it. He was still dressed in all black, but this time he wore a long-sleeved T-shirt, fitted enough to hint at the strong torso underneath. He was tall, his head nearly reaching the top of the doorframe.

As he turned, closing the door behind him, our eyes met. He paused for a second and then stepped up to the foot of my bed, resting one hand on the railing. He watched me with a neutral expression on his face. I watched him back, not feeling at all awkward about maintaining eye contact with a complete stranger for so long. A scar cut through the middle of his right eyebrow, and a black-and-gray tattoo was peeking out of the black fabric at his neck.

"How you feeling?" His voice was firm, forceful, but it still felt like honey washing over me.

My own voice was groggy, though clear enough in the silent room. "You pulled me out of the water." I didn't bother answering his question. It wasn't important at that moment.

"No. My colleague did. I pulled you into the chopper."

He wasn't going to insist I focus on my health, on getting better, on getting my strength up—all those empty things people insisted when they were trying to avoid speaking about the difficult things. The important things. *Good.*

"You sat with me. I could hear your voice. Even over the engine."

"Yes . . ." He looked away briefly before meeting my gaze again, letting the word trail off. As if he was going to add more but decided not to.

"Only the copilot and I made it. There were no other survivors?" I had to be sure. I had to hear someone say it.

"No." His answer was definitive, but his eyes narrowed slightly, wondering whom I was asking about. Whom I had lost.

I screwed my eyes shut, fisting the hospital sheets in my weak fingers.

My mother . . .

My mother was on the plane with me.

There were no other survivors.

She was not a survivor. She was . . . she . . .

"My mother." I opened my eyes as I said it.

His face fell when the two words left my mouth. He lifted his other hand to the railing of my bed and leaned heavily on the utilitarian gray plastic, hanging his head. He swore under his breath and started breathing hard.

Why was he so upset?

I had so many questions. *What happened? Why did the plane crash? How did no one else survive? Why did I make it? Why not her? How did you know where to search? Where am I? What's going to happen now? Who are you? Why are you still here? Why do you care?*

But I couldn't find it in me to care about the answers.

No. That one little word had confirmed what I had suspected since I'd first woken up, with a stranger sitting in the chair at my bedside instead of my mother.

I'd felt strong when I'd woken up a few moments earlier, but now I felt weak again. An awful pressure built in my chest, and a lump formed in my throat.

She was gone. Forever. I would never see my mother again. Never speak to her, hug her, argue with her. *Argue.* That was the last thing we'd done. She died thinking I was mad at her.

I was alone in the world. I was motherless. An orphan. I had felt lonely for much of my life, but whatever my mother's reasons were for keeping us distant from other people, she had always been there for me. She was the one constant in my life, the one person I could always rely on.

Yes, I had felt lonely in the past, but lying in that hospital bed with a stranger at my bedside, I truly knew what it meant to feel *alone*.

I'm alone.

Fat tears finally overflowed, and I wrapped my arms around my torso. I began to sob as I rolled onto my side toward the window, every muscle in my body taut with despair.

Boots squeaked across the linoleum, and then the thin hospital blanket was pulled over my shoulder. The bed behind me dipped, and his body pressed into mine from behind, his arm snaking around my front. He held me tight and I heard his voice, close to my ear.

"You are not alone."

I must have said that out loud. His declaration made me cry harder—ugly, unrestrained tears. Sobs wracked my body as I curled into a ball.

He held on to me through it all. We didn't touch, nowhere did our skin make contact, but he held me tight until my crying calmed down to soft sobs. He held me tight as the sobs gave way to silent tears pooling on the pillow. He held me tight as I drifted off into blissful unconsciousness again.

When I woke up the next morning, there was a nurse at the foot of my bed, writing something on a clipboard, and the stranger really was gone.

Keep reading! https://geni.us/variant-lost

ABOUT THE AUTHOR

Kaydence Snow has lived all over the world but ended up settled in Melbourne, Australia. She lives near the beach with her husband.

She draws inspiration from her own overthinking, sometimes frightening imagination, and everything that makes life interesting. She believes sarcasm is the highest form of wit and has the vocabulary of a highly educated, well-read sailor. When she's not writing, thinking about writing, planning when she can write next, or reading other people's writing, she loves to travel and learn new things.

To keep up to date with Kaydence's latest news and releases sign up to her newsletter here:

kaydencesnow.com/#newsletter

Join her reader group here:

facebook.com/groups/KaydenceSnowLodge

Or follow her on:

BY KAYDENCE SNOW

The Evelyn Maynard Trilogy

Variant Lost

Vital Found

Vivid Avowed

The Complete Evelyn Maynard Trilogy

Devilbend Dynasty

Like You Care

Like You Hurt

Like You Should

Like You Know

Standalones

Just Be Her

It Started With a Sleigh

Sand and Secrets

Reverie and Redemption

Expose Me